WILD LOVE

BOOK 4 IN THE MERMAIDS OF CORNWALL SERIES

BY

AMAYA HART

A HUGE THANK YOU TO MY READERS FOR TAKING A CHANCE ON ME.

TABLE OF CONTENTS

'I must be a mermaid. I have no fear of depths and a great fear of shallow living'

Anais Nin

1

Two people walked leisurely on the beach along the lips of the lapping waves, against the soft orange of the horizon, and the sun, a drowsy ball of red, gradually slipped behind the farthest edge of the ocean. The stars had begun waking, popping out without order, little blotches stuck to the sky. They twinkled happily, as though they admired the lovers at the beach, walking, bumping into each other, and laughing.

"You're very funny, Adian," Vanessa said, all giggles, remnants of a course of laughter only moments ago, falling out her mouth.

Adian let his lips curve into a little smile.

They were walking together, hands entwined like twigs, their feet sinking into the soft wet sand of the beach.

"Do you ever feel the sea calling out to you? Like each time, it dances, or laps at the beach, it's a voice drawing you in?" Vanessa asked.

Adian looked out into the sea.

"Yes", he said. "Every time. That's why I choose to watch the sunset and the sunrise here. Where the sea would sing my soul to a perfect calm, as the view of the sun, setting or rising, placates my sense of sight. I've not seen anything more beautiful. Except you."

He placed his eyes on Vanessa, taking her in. Her wavy black hair, dancing in light spasms as the sea breeze combed through it, her lips, full and possessive of a certain succulence, her eyes soulful and captivating. She was what one got when the beauty of sunset and the sea were put together.

Vanessa felt like a warmth had burst in her heart, sending a chill through to her entire body. The edges of her lips itched, until they spread, forming a smile.

Adian curved his arm around her waist, and pulled her to him. Vanessa stared into his eyes, letting them engage her. Then she closed hers as Adian brought his face closer for a kiss.

It had been eight months since Vanessa had almost drowned, since the attack from Quintess' guards. Adian, Elan, and Ervin had put hands together to repel them, and had given the Celtic Sea an offering of bodies.

Eight months and the love between Adian and Vanessa had blossomed into a forest of beautiful possibilities. They had grown to understand that strange energy that had sprang like vines whenever they were together. It was the link between their souls. A consummation of who and what they were. It was love.

They broke out of the kiss, and their eyes burned with life, as the crash of waves serenaded them.

They walked up after some time, climbing out of the beach and on to the hills, at the edge of which sat the cottage.

"How I wish they were around", Vanessa said.

"Huh?" Adian replied, blinking rapidly, as though he had just been baptized with a bucket of water.

"Rosie and Olivia, I wish they were home?"

"Where'd they go?"Adian said.

"They went to visit their grandparents, and also to spread out invitations for Olivia and Ervin's wedding."

There was a slight pause before Adian spoke again.

"I do know that Ervin and Elan are around though."

Vanessa flung her eyes to the porch, then to the sides of the cottage. Nothing.

"How'd you know they are around?" Vanessa asked.

Adian smiled, mischief gleaming through the white of his teeth.

"I've developed the power of telepathy." He replied. "I picked their thoughts from inside the house."

Vanessa laughed. Then looked at Adian, her eyes heavy with taunting.

"If you really can read minds, then tell me. What am I thinking right now?"

Adian chuckled.

"Trust me. You don't want me to." He said.

"Trust me. I want you to." Vanessa replied.

"Are you sure you want me rummaging your mind? I'll unearth all your little secrets."

"Knock yourself out."

Adian smiled. Then he let his lids shut over his eyes. And attempted to concentrate. Soon, his eyelids had tightened, forming wrinkles, as though he were straining against a psychic force or wall, or something.

He opened them, and affected heavy gasps.

"I didn't know you were this strong." He said. "How did you build such a psychic wall?"

Vanessa *pfft*-ed.

"Mister, if you had even the smallest seed of telepathy, you would have gleaned from my thoughts that Ervin and Elan are atop the cottage working on the roof, as they have been for some time now, and that they've just seen us."

Adian laughed and lifted his arms slowly into the air.

"You've caught me." He said in between laughter.

"What are you two up to?" Ervin called out.

Vanessa and Adian looked up to him at almost the same time. And a smile split across their faces.

"Hello, Ervin." Vanessa greeted.

"Hello", Ervin replied. "How's our boy, Adian, doing?"

"Let's say I'm not the one stuck on a roof, and facing the risk of breaking a leg or something," Adian replied, a huge grin on his face.

Ervin and Elan laughed.

"Nessa", Elan called, looking down at them.

"Elan", Vanessa called.

"I can see Adian has taken you on another tour of the sunset, hasn't he?"

Vanessa laughed.

They exchanged light banter for a short time, before waving each other goodbyes.

On their way through the dirt path that led to the major road which they would take to go home, Adian could not help but wonder how quickly the sides of a leaf could turn. He still had them, visited them sometimes – memories of when he and Elan were at loggerheads. He had understood Elan's hostility towards him. He had tried to kill Rosie more than once. However, he had apologised and sought to make things right after he had been racked with heavy showers of guilt. But Elan would have none of it. Not until they had saved Vanessa from the attack on the beach.

He remembered expending the full force of the power tugging inside him, and had been swallowed into the bowels of darkness in return. When he awoke, he found himself in the sister's cottage, cemented his love with Vanessa, and was reconciled with Elan.

"Why are you smiling?" Vanessa asked, looking curiously at Adian.

"Huh?"

"You had a smile on your face just now."

"Oh. That. I was just thinking, you know, of how different things were between Elan and I. And how things are now."

Vanessa smiled, and bumped slightly into Adian.

"Don't you feel glad?" she asked.

"Me?" Adian asked. "Very glad. I feel very glad. Now I can take care of you and also help watch after Rosie and her sister."

"Aaaaw. Isn't that cute?" Vanessa asked, touching the sides of his face with her fingers.

Adian smiled. Then he scooped Vanessa up from the ground.

Vanessa squealed and then fell into a bout of laughter. Adian carried her, with little effort, towards the approaching dusk.

2

Sarina came out of the kitchen stirring a cup of coffee. Steam from the cup rose up in curly wisps, and assailed her nostrils. She sniffed, taking in the smell of coffee and *ahh*-ed. She liked her coffee black with just the touch of sugar. Outside, London was alive with the swish of fleeting cars, honking, the ding of bicycle bells, and the knock of shoe-*d* feet on the cobbled walkways. She sank into a couch, sipped, and let her ears drink up and savour, the sound of the city wafting into the tiny apartment through the windows.

She leaned into the couch, and closed her eyes, letting herself be serenaded by the melody of London, and the comforting taste of coffee, on her tongue.

Then there was a knock on the door, breaking Sarina's state of zen. Her eyes flew open. She waited. Then the knock came a second time. This time, a bit louder than before.

"Who's there?" Sarina asked, her voice, a few chords away

from a shrill soprano.

Silence. And then another knock.

"Hold on," Sarina said, dropping her almost empty cup on the small coffee table before her.

She stood from the couch, and walked to the door. At the door, she thought she could hear the hum of low voices, and giggling. She opened the door, and was hit by a wave of "Surprise!", then a hail of laughter.

Sarina looked at the laughing girls. First, she was surprised. Then she felt joy stretch out from inside her, like a growing sapling.

"Olivia! Rosie!" she yelled.

She rushed towards them and welcomed the both of them into a tight embrace.

She broke out from the hug. The three of them stood out there, within the little confines of the rail fencing, and took themselves in.

"What are you girls doing here?" Sarina asked, her eyes effulgent with surprise.

"It's good to see you too, Sarina," Rosie said.

Sarina groaned. Olivia laughed.

"Can't you see she's glad enough?" Olivia asked Rosie in between laughter.

Rosie laughed.

"Enough of the laughing you two", Sarina said.

Sarina looked out to the busy street in front of her, and to both sides of her ground-floor terrace apartment. The three of them standing out there were not attracting any kind of stares.

"Please come inside. We don't want the attention of the entire London on ourselves, now do we?"

She turned and walked inside. Rosie and Olivia stood out for a moment, and looked around. Taking in the pots of flowers, standing in rows, along the sides of the fence.

"It's good to see some things are still the same," Rosie said, her voice low like the hum of a bee.

"Yeah", Olivia said.

"You girls coming in?" Sarina asked, popping her head out through the yawning doorway.

"Yeah, yeah, we are." They chorused and walked towards the door.

Inside, Rosie and Olivia placed their bags on a stool and dropped carelessly into the couch. The sound of closing cupboards, and clattering, wafted out of a little door.

"Sarina", Olivia called. "You really don't have to do that."

"At least not immediately," Rosie said, her voice laced with plea.

Sarina's head popped out the door.

"You girls have not the faintest idea of what you're talking about. Coffee, yes?"

Her head went back in, not waiting for an answer.

Rosie and Olivia let their eyes roam around the living room.

The living room was a small space, about half of their living room back at Cliffside. Grey wallpapers with vines of silver flowers weaving seamlessly into each other, like rivulets of water, clothed the entire wall. There was one couch and an armchair in the living room, and a small fireplace nested at the end wall. There was a shelf, with a television, a DVD player, and rows of discs. A rug ran over the entire floor, soft, and soothing, like tufts of wool to the under of Rosie and Olivia's feet. All in all, the room was compact and full, not like the teeth of maize on a cob, but like a tree with fruits.

"Okay, girls," Sarina said, walking hurriedly into the living room, a tray in her hand. This contained coffee and carrot cake. Then she placed the tray on the small table, before Rosie and Olivia. The cups on the tray chinked, and concentric ripples sprang from the middle of the coffee in the cups, spreading to the edges.

"You didn't have to bother yourself, Sarina." Rosie groaned.

"Our visit was intended as a surprise. And…"

"And now", Sarina interrupted, "I'm the one giving you girls the surprise."

Rosie and Olivia laughed.

Sarina walked back to the kitchen and came back in, with a plate of cheese and cucumber sandwiches.

Soon, they all chewed, sipped their coffee, chewed, and sipped again.

"Woah", Sarina said. "Didn't know you girls were this hungry. Allow me to make some more sandwiches."

"No, No, No", they said, their voices, a chaotic weave of sounds.

"Fine. Now you girls should spill. Tell me what you've both been up to."

"Uhm… There's nothing major actually," Olivia replied looking at Rosie.

"Come on", Sarina said. "My cousins visit me after such a long time, and there are no tales?"

"Well, to start with", Rosie began. She cast a glance at Olivia, who flicked her eyes away, and pretended to admire the flower vase sitting on one of the sills to the windows looking out to the street. "We've just been to see Grandpa Alex."

"You did?" Sarina asked.

"Yes," Rosie replied.

"And I was only there to see him last week. Oh, how he made me laugh till my ribs ached."

"Typical Grandpa Alex for you." Olivia quipped in smiling.

Rosie smacked her lips together.

"Okay… so we were in his place, extending an invite to Oly's wedding."

It took moments for the meaning of the words to hit Sarina. First, she was numb, her brain whirring and clicking, eating up the bits of data, digesting them, and then…

Her eyes perked up. They shone with meaning, with understanding, with happiness. She squealed with excitement. Then looked at Olivia.

"You're getting married. Goodness me! That's exceedingly great news." She said.

They began to chatter, exchanging jokes and comments about Olivia's fiance. Sometimes, Olivia would step into the defensive, speaking of how incredibly good-looking and exciting Ervin was, and would arouse a burst of laughter from Rosie and Sarina. Then, without any nautical direction in mind, they steered off light chatter and into talks of themselves, their powers, and of mermaid-*ry*.

"Wait", Sarina said, leaning out of the couch, and drawing closer to its edge. "What did you say?"

Rosie gulped and flashed Olivia a look.

"What we're trying to say is this. You know how growing up, we always stood out with our powers? We always had this thing, this extraordinary ability about us that was uncommon. Like we were strange, weirdoes, that sort of thing."

Sarina's mind brought up a few memories. In some of them, there were little Rosie and Olivia, with little her, sitting ducks for the suspicious stares they got from other kids. In others, it was just her. One of them was at a swimming pool; she had just participated in a class contest and had come first. She had dove into the pool, went through the water, and popped out at the other side, only to discover that she had given the rest of her classmates a wide berth. Chants of 'weirdo' had hit her from the sides. Some of her co-contestants had even accosted her.

She blinked, returning to the present.

Rosie was still talking.

"… we'd grown not really knowing what we were, but careful enough not to divulge it to everyone, except trusted people. Till one day, a body washed up on our beach."

"What?" Sarina asked, her eyes the size of tennis balls. "You mean like a body, body?"

"Yes." Olivia said. "Ervin"

Rosie cleared her throat and ran a finger across her hairline before continuing.

"We took him into our home and took care of him. There was something strange about him from the start. The cuts, the bruises. But not just that. There were other things. Magical. Like silver bracelets coming out of nowhere. But we couldn't get answers at first."

"Why was that?" Sarina asked.

"He had lost his memories when he hit his head close to the cliffs."

"Oh", Sarina said.

"Then Oly almost drowned. And he dove into the sea to rescue her. That's when the aura of mystery surrounding him burst. He was a merman, and began recovering his memories as soon as he had transformed."

Sarina listened, with rapt attention, her mind running along as Rosie narrated. It was as though Sarina was there with her, wanted to be there with her. Rosie spoke of a dream, going to Dublin, stringing a harp, being followed, almost being killed. Then her transformation. And Olivia's transformation. Almost losing her friend to guards of some witch queen controlling the sea. And now, Olivia's wedding.

Sarina took this all in, like she was a sponge under a trickle of water. Except that in her case, she did not let the water flow out. She held bits of the information Rosie had churned out, let them gather, until they coalesced into a whole, a tangible meaning. Something clicked, somewhere within the recesses of Sarina's being. Like there had been a dislocation in the joints that made her life, and now the loose joint had just popped into place. She stared and stared, her eyes needles, piercing through the fabric of space. She stared until a trickle of happiness seeped out from inside her. Then the trickle grew into rivulets, streams, and then a gushing fountain. Her face flushed with mirth and was creamed with a radiant smile.

"It all makes sense now." She said, her voice many bits higher than before.

Her eyes flew from Rosie to Olivia. The sisters were a bit surprised at the way Sarina had taken the news. She had accepted it like a cake would accept a knife through it. Without resistance. Without questions.

"I'm a… mermaid", she thought. That explained the uncanny happenings in her life stronger than any conjecture she had ever cooked up. The strange pull the ocean always had on her. The emotions the sea seemed to trigger in her every time she stood close by it.

She looked towards the sisters. Then she got up and paced around her living room with the sisters watching her. She felt bubbles of elation welling up from within. The walls of the living room seemed to draw closer and closer, within each other from the movement she made. Until she dropped into the armchair.

"Tell me about it?" she asked. "Tell me. I want to know more about mermaids."

Rosie gave Olivia a 'would-you-like-to-try' look. Olivia gave her a stern look that said 'no'. Rosie turned, and let the words flow out. Everything she could remember and could say about mermaids. Sarina was a good listener as Rosie told her about Dublin and the harp.

Shortly before they left, they got into talking about life in Cliffside. Rosie made mention of her booming sea shell business, and the amount of tourists it attracted from outside. And how the entire village had been injected with a dose or two of life. They talked some more about other little things. Like how Sarina was faring in the big city, and all that.

Then, like all things, their visit came to its close.

"I think we still have more places to stop by in London, before we show the big city our behinds," Olivia said.

They all laughed.

Sarina walked them up to her little metal gate, bid farewell with a hug to each of them, and watched them walk down the cobbled way until they flagged down a taxi and got in.

Sarina walked back into the apartment and shut the door behind her. Since she had bade her cousins goodbye, Sarina had been looking for sheets of things, she could use to cover the feeling of forlornness that was growing like a hump inside her. It was as though they had detached the meaning they had elucidated to her, leaving her with only the shadow of the light they had brought.

Sarina picked up the empty cups and plates from the table and walked into her kitchen. The kitchen was a little cube, like a quarter of the living room, but it served. Comfortably well. She dropped the plates in the sink, opened the tap and let the water run over the plates. The running water made a slight splashing sound as it hit the plates. Droplets of water jumped out from the splash, adorning Sarina's hand with specs of wetness. Sarina let the water run and run, until it began to hold a particular allure for her. Slowly, and purposefully, her hand rose, like it had a mind of its own. Then it moved slowly through the air, floating as above water, till her fingers pierced the stream of water falling out the tap. The water was soft, and warm, bathing her fingers with a refreshing wetness. And all it did was remind Sarina that she was a mermaid.

She switched off the tap. A gurgling sound erupted from beneath the cluster of plates and cups, as the water went down the sink's drain. Sarina wiped her wet hands on her black leggings, and walked out of the kitchen. She paced the living room once, twice, thrice. Then she went in another door, one that led to her bedroom. She collapsed into bed, and let her eyes trace the lines on the ceiling.

Sarina's mind was spinning, making weaves, discarding what it had weaved, and making new weaves. She rolled in her bed, ruffling the blankets and rolled again. She closed her eyes. Sarina could not go on carrying out her normal activities, living as though she had not heard what Rosie and Olivia had said. She was from

18

the ocean, and that was the life she wanted to live.

Sarina sat up from the bed, her eyes shining with a rigid new light.

3

Three weeks later, Rosie, Olivia, and Vanessa are sat at the kitchen table, helping themselves to buttered toasted crumpets, when there was a knock on the door.

"Who's there?" Rosie asked, looking at Olivia.

There was a muffled response from the door.

Rosie got to her feet, the wooden chair she sat on making a scraping sound as she pushed it back.

"Hold on", she called.

The door clicked as Rosie turned the knob, taking the lock in. She opened the door, and her face flushed with surprise. There standing before her, wearing a large travel rucksack and holding a suitcase, was Sarina.

"Hello", Sarina greeted, a smile decorating her face.

The surprise on Rosie's face fueled the amusement Sarina felt, until she had a stupid grin on her face.

"Sarina", Rosie said, and then blinked, recovering herself. "Please do come in", she said, stepping out to the porch, and helping Sarina with her suitcase.

Sarina was hit by a light wave of dizziness, brought about by the unfamiliarity of the cottage. She almost lost her footing, but she winced as if she wanted to squeeze out the feeling of dizziness. She knew that this cottage once belonged to Grandpa Alex, but had had no cause to visit it in the past. The living room was large and sparsely occupied. A direct opposite of hers in London.

Sarina heard someone call her name. She looked and saw Olivia approaching her. Olivia's arms opened, like the petals of a flower, and Sarina went into the embrace. There was another girl, trailing behind Olivia, Sarina noticed. She had long dark curly hair that fell just past her shoulders.

"Sarina", Rosie said, "meet Vanessa, a very close friend of ours, about the closest". Rosie pointed at the girl with the dark hair. "Vanessa, meet Sarina, our cousin."

Sarina noticed how warm Vanessa's smile was. She gave a smile of her own, but she could tell that it did not match Vanessa's in any way.

"It's nice meeting you, Vanessa", Sarina greeted, shaking Vanessa's hand.

"It's nice to meet you too," Vanessa replied warmly.

Soon Sarina sat at the kitchen table with Rosie, Olivia, and

Vanessa munching on a toasted crumpet.

"I'm sorry for the quality of the meal, Sarina," Rosie said. "Everyone's busy running around for Olivia's wedding. There's no time to cook. As we speak to you the guys, Adian, Elan, and Ervin are out in the sea, looking for shells and pearls to weave into Oly's wedding dress."

"It's okay", Sarina said, smiling just before she took another bite out of her crumpet.

"Besides", Olivia said, "Isn't it a bit early to be coming now for the wedding? Arrivals aren't due for some time."

Sarina was silent for a moment. Then she *hmm*-ed.

Her eyes ran from Rosie to Olivia and back to Rosie. Then she spoke, as though she were rolling a boulder off her shoulders.

"I did it."

Rosie, Olivia, and Vanessa flashed each other a look. Confusion danced in their eyes like a screen of smoke.

"Did what, Sarina?" Olivia asked, leaning further into the table.

"I strung the harp," Sarina said. She spoke as though she was spitting hot food from her mouth.

"What!" Rosie exclaimed. Her chair creaked, as she jerked.

Olivia's eyes were glowing balls that could not contain the surprise of what she had just heard.

Slowly, and gradually, what was once surprise coating their

eyes and face, turned into worry. Rosie and Olivia looked at themselves. Their eyes became portals, sparking into existence a chain of communication between themselves, and passing across meaning. Then they looked away. Back to Sarina. Vanessa gleaned from the looks in their eyes, and from her experience that what Sarina did was far from good and beautiful. It was dangerous, plain and outright.

"It's a good thing you came here, Sarina," Olivia said.

Sarina let her eyes swallow Olivia, and let the fact of what she had said settle in her mind. This was probably the most pleasant thing she had heard since the days following her stringing the harp in Dublin.

Rosie nodded in affirmation to what Olivia had said.

"But then there's something else that you need to know. First of all, we must ask you to do something for us."

"What's that?" Sarina asked.

Olivia flashed Rosie another look, and spoke.

"I'd like for you to narrate to us your experience with the harp. Like the events surrounding stringing it. And what happened after you had strung it. You can be as detailed as you want to be. We've got like all day."

"Well", Sarina began. "It was very uneventful."

"Pardon?" Rosie asked, her eyes candles flaming mild shock and surprise.

"I mean, there were no incidents in Dublin. I walked into the Long Room, and I met the harp, standing naked on its platform."

"What do you mean naked?" Rosie asked.

"Like there was no glass casing around it. There was nothing around it." Sarina replied.

Rosie and Olivia exchanged looks. This time their look was troubled.

"What's the problem?" Sarina asked. "I've been seeing the looks you two give each other. Is there a problem?"

Olivia cleared her throat.

"You see, Sarina, there's something we forgot to tell you when we were at your place."

"Okay..." Sarina said, nodding, and accepting the bits of information in stride.

"We didn't mention the harp guards."

"Harp guards?" Sarina asked. This time it was her turn to be confused.

"They are people, well mermen, who guard the harp," Olivia replied.

"Remember that witch queen we told you about?" Rosie asked.

"Yeah. The one that's called Quin-something, yes?"

"Yeah. Yes, that one." Rosie answered, and then continued.

"Well, she has mermen watching over the harp to ensure that the banished daughters of the sea, remain banished. In fact, Adian has now informed us that they are always watching within the busts of statues lining the aisle where the harp is kept. These guards are there, upon orders to kill any banished daughter who comes up to the harp to cure the curse."

"Well, not every one of them is bent on carrying out those orders." Vanessa interrupted. "Some of them are different. Like Adian."

Olivia and Rosie nod in affirmation.

"However," Vanessa continued, "it's best if you're wary and trustful of no one."

Sarina's eyes roved in their sockets.

"Well, I didn't see anybody." She said.

"And while coming here, you're sure you weren't followed?" Olivia asked.

"Followed?" Sarina asked. "Followed?" Her eyes were wide now. "Is this that serious?"

"Yes, Sarina. It is." Olivia replied. "In fact, Rosie and I got followed. We had a face-off with a group of them some eight months ago. It was a face-off that revolved around life or death."

"Wow", Sarina mouthed, and leaned into the table.

"But the witch Queen isn't the only one with guards around the harp. There are good guards too. That's how Rosie met Elan. Elan had followed her from Dublin, protecting her all the way."

They talked for some time, taking care not to overemphasize, but also not underemphasizing, the notion of safety to Sarina. Then they dabbled into more light matters. The talk of Rosie and Elan moving into their just completed house, nesting not far from the cottage. Sarina smiled and wished Rosie a hearty congratulations.

It was a long way into the evening. The sun had come down considerably, and was now sending shafts of harsh light into the living room through the windows. Vanessa had left to go home. Rosie and Olivia had gone up to prepare Rosie's old room for Sarina. Sarina walked, slowly, around the living room. The soles of her shoes made an accompanying thump across the grey floorboards, while her eyes roamed the entire room. From its grey granite walls, to its fireplace, two or three times larger than hers, to the stairs that led up. It was while looking at the walls that she picked out the photos. They were in wooden frames, hanging, without any particular arrangement. Rosie and Olivia were in most of the frames, if not all. And they were almost never alone. In one, they were splashing in the water, in another, they were at the cliffs, in some, at the beach. Every time they smiled. Every time they were full of life. Sarina felt a faint longing rise inside her, a small sense of jealousy rear its head, at the lives Rosie and Olivia had with their attractive mermen.

Memories of her romantic life ballooned out the murk causing a jumble of other thoughts. Sarina felt sad and solemn. As far as she could remember, she had always been unlucky with love. Her mind rewound, travelling back in time to a few days ago.

Her mind had still been hyperactive, thrilled, from her experience at Dublin. Everything had gone almost as Rosie had described. She had seen the book with the golden spine, unhooked the chain from around it, and brought it down. As soon as she had flipped over its thick metallic cover, the pages began to flip by themselves. Her heart had pounded, her mind agog with wonder, her eyes orbs filled with awe. This was magic. And she was witnessing it firsthand. It was as though, the book was in tune with her mind. No matter how slow she read, or how fast, or how she reread certain line or paragraphs, the pages would turn over only after she was done reading them. The book told her more than Rosie and Olivia had.

The book shut with a snap when it had told her enough. Then, gradually, it assumed a crystalline hue, becoming transparent, until it shimmered out of existence.

Sarina remembered exhaling deeply. She had never been so thrilled in her life. This short encounter with the supernatural was incentive enough to make her envy her cousins. It burned in her, fossil to the fuel of her passion, egging her into the life of the extraordinary. Her eyes flew to the harp on the pedestal.

Sarina walked towards it, in careful, respectful steps. She felt like she was standing before something of greater value than her own existence. The strings were thin, taut, and shinier than the rest of the harp. Sarina had stretched her fingers. Her heart throbbed filling her ears with pulsations. Her fingers moved further in towards the harp. She took one more step. Then her fingers touched the strings. At first, there was no sensation of the feel of the strings to the tip of her fingers. Then she let her fingers run. Immediately, tremors ran through her fingers, and travelled down the rest of her body. She felt a strange electrifying tingle throughout her body, even after she had withdrawn her hand to herself. She threw one more look at the harp, and knew that this was all this mystic object would do. It was time to go. She looked around. There were rows and rows of shelves, busts of statues, and other protected items. But nobody. She had walked out the Long Room, her face affixed with a smile, unable to contain the joy bubbling within.

The flight from Dublin to London was uneventful. Yet each time Sarina looked out the windows, she sought to hang with the whiff of clouds, floating in colonies in the air. When she got off the train at London St Pancras station, she had flagged down a taxi, almost singing her destination to him. Her boyfriend who she lived with would be waiting, she knew. Ruffled brown hair, looking like a million hummingbirds were making love in it, large grey eyes, ensconced behind thick glasses, and baggy clothes, Robert struck the perfect nerdy figure. Still, he carried this aura with him, a childishness, a carelessness for things to come, and it seemed to sit well with Sarina.

She had imagined the surprise that would bloom on his face when he opened the door to see her standing there. The prospect alone, made her feel like a child who had just made its first sandcastle. She had not given him an exact return date.

Getting to their apartment, she had raised her hand to knock, when she was restrained by a new thought. *Why not just walk in on him? It'll make the surprise greater.*

Sarina had smiled. Dug her hand into one of the pockets lining the lower side of her jacket, and brought out keys. She had tried unlocking the door, as stealthily as she could. She succeeded. Except for little clicks. Which she gave off as inconsequential.

Her living room greeted her, with a blank stare. Everything was as she had left it. Except for maybe the size. Sarina felt like it had grown smaller, constricting like a noose. She walked in, and had opened her mouth to call out for Robert when she was hit by the first of the sounds. It was low, almost inaudible, and it came in short intermittent breaks. Sarina's brows had furrowed, her eyelids almost touching together, as she strained her senses to get the better of what the sound was or where it was coming from. She received one of the answers soon enough. The sound climbed a sharp peak. It was still low, but it was louder than previous ones.

Sarina's eyes flew towards the door that led to her bedroom. That's where the sound was coming from. She walked, cautiously, letting each feet sink into the softness of the rug, before lifting it. The door to her bedroom was slightly open. There was a thin line of light, shining from the room, between the edge of the door and the post. She pushed it open, tentatively, and her heart banged against her chest. It was like thunder had struck in a single massive peal of rage. Sarina staggered back. Lips trembling, fingers twitching, eyes watering. She could not get her eyes off the girl, naked, and sweaty, grinding atop of Robert. She staggered back till she hit the wall in a thud. Just then, Robert's head flew her way.

"Christ!" he screamed, pushing the girl from atop him, and gathering the bed covers to him to hide his nakedness.

"Sarina. Sarina, I can explain. It's not as grave as you see it." He said.

Sarina could not hear anything, or see anything. It was all hurt inside her. She shut her eyes, and then made a swift decision. She walked into the room, ignoring Robert's calls and explanations, ignoring the girl who had begun to rummage the bed for her clothes. Sarina opened her wardrobe and began to throw things into a suitcase. Olivia and Rosie had been the only people she could think of. The only protective gauze she could wrap around herself and prevent the pain from eating her up.

Now she was here. Still feeling the hangover from the collapse of her relationship. But bolstered by the hope of better things.

Right now she looked forward to Olivia's wedding. She was not sure of what she would do, or what would happen to her after then, but she made up her mind to immerse herself, fully, without reservations of any sort, into the pools of distractions Olivia's wedding and the preparations would present. Besides, she had Rosie and Olivia to keep her company. She was sure that the warmth of their companionship would envelop her, sluicing away all the sadness and unease stuck to her person.

"Sarina", a voice called.

Sarina turned. It was Rosie. She was standing at the bottom of the stairs. Wisps of her auburn hair had strayed from the family tucked behind in a ponytail, and draped over her face. Yet, it did not obscure the warmth that exuded from her smile. Sarina smiled in return.

"You should come upstairs," Rosie said.

Sarina followed after Rosie, leaving the living room, a large, almost empty space. Soon a squeal of delight pierced the silence the entire house boasted.

4

Sarina's eyes fluttered open, like the wings of butterflies. Her body was enveloped in the smooth folds of bed sheets, and the soft depression of the bed. Sarina sat up, and yawned. A smile burst on her face. She finally had an idea of what heaven was. Living in a house close to the sea was it. From her room upstairs, she could hear the swash of the waves as they crashed onto shore, or against the cliffs. The breeze that smoothed its way in through the window carried the fresh smell of the sea. Powerful and pleasant. And that was not all. Within the sea-breeze, sweet scents of flowers thread themselves, creating an immaculate sensation. Sarina *ahh*-ed, slid her feet into her green slippers, and walked towards the window, looking out to a portion of the hills.

The hills stretched out before her, uneven folds, spread with the green of tall, even grass, and stalks of beautiful flowers, swaying with the wind, like intoxicated worshippers dancing in veneration. She followed the hills until they rose stealthily and then dropped into the sea.

"Cliffs", Sarina thought.

There were birds, some so little they could fit comfortably within a closed fist, and others were large, as large as normal birds. These little ones fleeted among the green of the hills, going from flower to flower, and singing gaily. The large ones walked through the green, pecking at the earth.

Sarina felt like she was flowing out her body, in wispy streams, and melding into the scene before her. She felt the sea tug at her soul. Then there was a rap on the door, and her ecstasy was cut short.

"Sarina", a voice called.

Sarina turned her head towards the door, her hand still resting on the window sill.

"Yeah", she answered.

"You up?"

"Sort of." She replied.

She did not know who, in particular, was speaking to her. Rosie? Olivia? The sisters' voices, if it differed, did only by a few minor notes.

"Just came to tell you that breakfast's ready."

"Yeah? What's for breakfast?" Sarina asked.

"Why don't you come and see?"

Sarina decided to step out into the small corridor.

"Rosie?" she called.

"Yeah?"

"Nothing. Just wanted to know who I was speaking with."

"Okay", Rosie said.

"Just give me a few minutes to prepare. I'll be down soon."

"Ok."

Sarina heard the low falls of Rosie's feet, reducing as she walked away from the bottom of the stairs. Sarina closed her eyes, sighed, and then walked towards the mirror in her room. Her reflection stared back. Large brown eyes, ruffled long dyed blue hair. Sarina wondered if the girl in the mirror could feel emotions. Its flare, burn, thrill. Spreading her fingers, she fixed them into her hair, like a comb, and shook it. Her hair danced, as her hand moved. Then Sarina cast her eyes on the table on which the mirror stood. The table was peopled by makeup, hair bobbles, bottles, and a host of other cosmetic items. Her eyes rummaged through the items, until they found what they were looking for. A hair clip. Running her palms across her hair, she stretched it back until it pulled into a tail. Then she clutched the tail, with one hand, twister the length and clipped it with the other. She took one more look at the mirror. She was good. Okay. No signs of a heartbreak from a crashed relationship. She shrugged. Her visit to Cliffside was beginning to take effect. She threw on a black t-shirt and some snug blue jeans.

She went into the bathroom and brushed her teeth. On her way down the stairs, she picked the light sound of chatter. The sound grew as she descended. Then there was a wave of laughter just as she came into the living room.

The kitchen table had several chairs evenly spaced around it, and there sat was Rosie and Olivia, who were joking, and laughing.

Rosie turned. And their eyes met. Sarina walked towards them, a smile building on her face, and sat.

With each tick of the clock, they would stab at the food on their plates, talk, chew, drink, laugh and stab at their food again.

Later, Sarina and Olivia huddled around Rosie. There were two baskets on the kitchen table. One was filled with colourful bits of shells arranged in loops – necklaces. The other was empty. Rosie began counting the necklaces. Picking from the full basket, and dropping it into the empty one for every necklace she counted.

"They're beautiful", Sarina crooned, picking one up and putting it to her slender neck.

"And it looks beautiful on you too", Rosie said, looking up from her counting. "You know, I and Elan would swim leagues into the sea to get shells of such unique quality."

"You mean you don't get these from the beach?" Sarina asked, her eyes a bit wider than before.

"From the beach?" Rosie asked. She laughed. "Nah. Elan once told me that the sea never gives up her beauties. You've got to put in some effort to procure what you want."

Sarina fingered the necklace. She seemed lost in thought.

"Uhm", Olivia cleared her throat, flicking Sarina out of her fascination. "Speaking of shells and the sea, I think it's time Sarina underwent total transformation. I don't think there'll be a better time."

"Yes. Yes, that's right." Rosie said, her voice in a high whine.

Sarina could feel her heart begin to make the first beats to a dance of apprehension. And still yet flowers of joy, from inside her, flung their petals open, letting pollen fly around, filling her with pleasantness. The unease she felt was probably a testament of untried things.

Rosie placed the almost empty basket on top of the full one and shifted it to the side of the table.

"Why don't you both go have a change of clothes? I'll wait down here. When you're done we'll go over to my place so I can grab some things, and then all roads lead to the beach."

"Excellent idea", Olivia said, her voice hunkered down by the strain of getting up from the couch.

Upstairs, Sarina browsed through her bag. Again and again. Then she sighed, closed her eyes, and ran her hand through her hair. In her haste, and cocoon of sorrow and hurt, she had forgotten to put in the essentials. Swimsuit.

36

"Who comes to a beachside, and doesn't come prepared?" she thought.

Just then a thought leapt into her mind.

She walked over to the wardrobe and flung the doors open. Rows of clothes dangled on hangers. She flicked each one to the side, looking and searching. Till she sighed, relief writing itself in obvious signs on her face.

About three swimsuits were hanging together in a group, that had been fashioned with a small silk skirt. Her eyes fell on the blue one, with an embroidery around its neckline of lighter blue. Sarina smiled.

5

Sarina came down the stairs with a turquoise dress thrown over her swimsuit. She had let her hair fall. So it shook lightly as she came down the stairs with a springy gait. Rosie looked up from her shells.

"Aaaaawn. You look so good." She said.

Sarina smiled.

"Where's Olivia?" she asked.

"She's been in and out her room, trying to settle on a swimsuit to wear."

Sarina nodded and made to speak, when Olivia walked in.

"I think this is best." She said, turning on her feet.

Sarina noticed how aptly the swimsuit and short nylon skirt clung to Olivia's curvy body. Like an airtight wrapping, it accentuated her curves, making it look like she had an extra layer of skin on.

"Definitely the best," Rosie said. "Now can we go?"

"One moment", Olivia said, running back through the door to her room.

Sarina sat and watched Rosie arranging her necklaces. The pile on the other basket was beginning to build up. The living room was too silent. Sarina flicked her eyes around and pushed herself further into the couch. She was feeling the tip of awkwardness' teeth begin to sink into her flesh.

"How's the business going?" Sarina asked, in a throwing-caution-to-the-wind sort of way.

"These?" Rosie asked, looking up. "It's doing well, very well. I don't mean to boast or anything, but, this is actually the reason why Cliffside's beginning to stir. Like the bulk of my customers are from outside Cliffside. Tourists, simple people who just saw my work and want to try it out for themselves, people who just come down here for the peace and reprieve the quiet of Cliffside offers. Elan and I, we built our house mostly from the proceeds."

Sarina mouthed an astonished 'wow'.

"And here I was thinking you can only make it in the big city." She mused.

"You mean London?" Rosie scoffed. "It's too noisy and busy. I don't think it would let simple innovations like this thrive. Like this is too dreamy for a place as practical. You get what I mean?"

"Absolutely," Sarina said.

Olivia walked in.

"Okay girls. We're good to go."

Sarina felt like she had burst out a bubble immediately she stepped out to the porch. Envelopes of the summer breeze, light and cool, buffeted her, making her hair writhe. The hillside rippled as its green danced with the breeze. They moved off the porch and moved a little to the left of the cottage, where Rosie's house sat twenty meters away. It was a bungalow. Not as big as the cottage, but gave off the impression that it was cosier, and less wasteful of space than the cottage. Plus, its wooden look, gave it the distinct aura of modernism, as opposed to the aged look of the cottage. As they climbed the short flight of stairs leading up to the door, there was the suspicion of a smile on Rosie's face. Olivia seemed to have noticed it, because she snickered.

"Wait for it." She said to no one in particular.

Rosie coughed lightly and then laughed. She got to the door, placed her fingers around the knob, and laughed some more.

The look on Sarina's face was between lost and amusement. She tasted a joke in the air. But she didn't know what exactly it was about.

Rosie saved her from wondering too much.

"Tell me, Sarina," she said intermittently, in between laughter, "if you're not before a house more better looking?"

Sarina's mind was beeping, processing, tying knots, and

connecting lines. Then it hit, like a pool ball rolling smoothly into a pocket. She turned towards the cottage and back to Rosie's house. Laughter burst out of her like an animal impatient to get into the open. Rosie laughed too. Olivia groaned exasperatedly. But as the laughter continued, the faint shadow of a smile appeared on her face.

"Okay, okay. The joke's over don't you think? Sarina, you should be the one putting more fire to Rosie's butt." Olivia said.

"Okay, okay", Sarina said, her voice still dripping with mirth.

The door came open with a series of clicks, and they poured into the living room. Rosie walked straight through a huge door at the end, while Olivia sank into a leather armchair. Sarina was more concerned with looking the living room over. She was enamoured with its simplicity. The wooden oak floor ran the length of the room. A simple silver chandelier hung tethered to the smooth white ceiling. There was a short tv stand on which sat a television, then on the lower rungs, a DVD player, and a neat cluster of DVDs and music records. The walls were clothed with imprints of trees on green earthy wallpaper. On one of the walls over the fireplace hung a huge photo on canvas – there stood by the setting sun on the water's edge were Elan, Ervin, Olivia, Rosie, Adian and Vanessa, all beaming with big smiles.

"Can't have enough of the magic, eh?''

Sarina turned abruptly, her hair swirling in a wide arc.

''Ervin's really gotten into photography, ever since Olivia gave him a camera for his birthday. He gave this to Elan and I, as a housewarming present''

Rosie was standing before her, simple, good-looking. She had on a short pink dress, more like a nightgown. Because it's sides hung away from her body. Rosie had braided her auburn hair. As Sarina looked closer she noticed Rosie holding a pearl in one hand. Before Sarina could ask what it was for Olivia stood up and hooked her arm in hers.

''Ready? Let's go''

Together they walked out the living room. The door shut with a bang, cutting off, in a single mouthful, the stream of air that had flowed in when it came open. There was a click. Then the sound of receding footsteps and jabbering voices.

6

The water was cool and silent. It wrapped around her chest seamlessly as she bobbed up and down. Sarina's arms waded through the water, as she kept herself still and afloat. She was alone. The only sound being the trickle of water down the bed of rocks that surrounded her. She had swam out, in tow of her cousins, to this section of the sea. They had followed the curve of the cliffs, going further and further away from the beach. Sarina had been fast. She had always been a fast swimmer and thus had garnered unusual name tags, and little friends. But her cousins were faster with their mermaid strength. They had woven in and out of the surface of the water, coming out with their heads, their back arching in a graceful curve, and their caudal fins the last thing to vanish into the bed of blue. Sarina just orchestrated a butterfly stroke that would have befuddled the minds of people, if her cousins were not there, in the water, with her.

Sarina turned to the sound of an echoed plop behind her. There was nothing.

"Probably drops of water", she thought to herself.

Sarina turned and turned. She was beginning to feel uneasy. Thoughts were building up in her mind, jumping on each other, and just when they had almost completed a cathedral of concern and fright. There was a loud splash in front of her. Rosie and Olivia had ballooned out the surface. Water dripped from their glossy hair, and exciting smiles sat on their faces.

"You girls took too long," Sarina said, her voice tilting towards crying. "I was beginning to think something had happened to you two."

"Sorry if we took long", Olivia said, "but what we went to get deserves the length of time we took as Rosie had accidentally dropped it."

Sarina looked from one cousin to the other.

Olivia looked at Rosie. Then she dug out a closed fist from the water. Stretching the clenched fist towards Sarina she unfurled her fingers to reveal a bright blue pearl, nesting in a bracelet woven from seaweed.

"What's this?" Sarina asked, her eyes, a slightly open mouth, sending out signals of confusion.

"It's for you," Olivia said, smiling.

"What?"

"Come on, just take it," Rosie said. "Or wait", she added, "We'll help you put it on."

They must have seen the look of confusion linger on Sarina's face, because just then Olivia oh-ed.

"I forgot." She said. "The pearl here", she rose the pearl closer to Sarina, while grazing it with her thumb, "helps with the transformation. I think it aids what the harp has already done."

Sarina flicked uncertain eyes towards Olivia.

"She's right," Rosie said, swimming closer. "At first, I'd returned from Dublin disappointed that there was no overt manifestation. Nothing. I was still human. It was not until Elan came around and revealed to us that there are pearls at the bottom of the sea, and these pearls, when on a mermaid's body, is the final step to her transformation."

She gave Sarina a get-it look.

Sarina nodded.

"Brace yourself," Olivia said, readying to place the bracelet around Sarina's wrist.

"Yeah", Rosie said, "the process is abrupt, but not entirely funny. Don't fret. It'll be over in a flash."

Sarina could feel her heart pound relentlessly, her pulse waltzing, her mind being bludgeoned with thoughts. She stretched forth her hand tentatively.

"Ready?" Olivia asked her.

She nodded.

She felt the smooth hardness of the woven weeds caress her hand, as they slipped over, and clasped over her wrist. Then…

7

Miles and miles away from them, further into the sea. The surface of the sea undulated, like a huge heavy blanket. The surface gave off glints of the sun, and a few fish poked around the surface. Probably for the feel of sunlight. Suddenly, they scattered. And just as quick as they darted away, something bigger burst out the surface. A man. A merman.

He had blonde hair that fell freely, wet and clumped, to the nape of his neck. He sent a sharp gust of air out of his mouth, sending droplets of water into the air. He turned his greenish-blue eyes, and looked further down the sea, towards land. There was something there. He could feel it. His intuition was bugging, just as it had been for some time now. He had learnt not to disobey, whenever his intuition bugged him.

He sank back into the sea and moved towards shore.

8

Asharp groan escaped Sarina. The world went stark white. Sarina felt like the bed of her mind, had split, burst into smithereens, revealing a new depth. A depth that had since existed, but was obscured by a layer of ordinariness, and humanness.

Rosie and Olivia watched, in open-mouthed awe. They imagined if it had been just this way for them. Beams of light shot out from Sarina's eyes and mouth, piercing the canopy of rock above them, and causing it to rain down in fist-sized chunks. Somehow, they plopped into the water, without touching any of them. Then the beam went out, as suddenly as it had come. Rosie and Olivia rushed to hold Sarina up, as she slouched.

Sarina's eyelids fluttered, then flew open. Her eyeballs had taken a shine. It was brown, coffee brown. But had now taken on a metallic hue. She looked around to find Rosie and Olivia's arms linked with hers. They looked at her with concern.

"What happened?" she asked, shrugging them away lightly.

Rosie and Olivia moved back slowly.

"You okay?" Olivia asked.

"Yeah," Sarina answered, then frowned a bit.

She felt a surprising but heavy sense of calm and peace, and comprehension. Like her mind had been a little garden and was now a large plantation. She felt stronger and stronger, like there was a pump inside her, bleeding out infinite reserves of energy.

Then her eyes fell to her sides, and startlingly, she noticed she could see a few feet beyond the surface. And that…

Sarina screamed.

Rosie and Olivia looked at themselves and smiled.

Sarina screamed again. Then laughed.

"I have a tail! I have a tail!" she screamed.

She twirled. Once, twice, thrice. Then she lifted her tail. Her caudal fin broke the surface of the water. Her tail was blue and had glimmering scales of silver.

Sarina had never felt so happy in her life. She felt accomplishment, fulfilment, a sense of purpose drizzle down on her, and settle, clinging to her like snow to the earth.

"Why don't we go for a swim?" Rosie suggested.

Olivia nodded.

"Hell yes!" Sarina squealed, swimming in a circle around Rosie and Olivia.

So they set out, slowly at first, creating mild ripples in their wake. As they left the bed of rocks further and further behind, Sarina's clumsy movements began to straighten out. Their speed increased and she kept pace.

"Okay," Rosie said, smiling. "You're getting better."

"I don't know girls. How about we take this underwater?"

"Yeah, yeah, absolutely, definitely", Sarina and Rosie chorused.

They dove under the water, milliseconds apart from each other. And all around them was blue, crystalline blue, and wetness. Without a cue, they began to swim, moving faster and faster. And faster and faster. Then with a concentric blast, Sarina shot forward like a bullet, leaving Rosie and Olivia in her wake. The sisters stopped, exchanged bewildered looks before, they shot forwards again. But try as they might, they could not catch up with Sarina. She was too fast.

Everything sped by in a blur of blue. Sarina felt an unending flow of energy within her. And she knew that no matter how fast she went, that energy could not be expended.

Sarina felt like she was living a dream. The dream. All this magic, the workings of the extra-ordinary, inosculated with her mind, creating the feel of a refreshing reality. Sarina saw this as the universe throwing her a new opportunity. An opportunity to start anew. To start as Sarina, the mermaid. She broke out to the surface, with such speed that she soared into the air. She took in the sun, an effulgent orb, with a circumference that melded into the azure of the sky. She somersaulted in the air, then fell back in with a splash. Then she broke the surface again. Gently, this time. Her mind spun back days ago. Those memories looked like they belonged, not just to a distant past, but to another life. She heard yelling from behind her. She turned and saw Rosie and Olivia speeding towards her.

Sarina smiled. Now she had family. Not just cousins, sisters.

"Holy crap, Sarina," Rosie called out, as they got closer.

"Yeah, wow," Olivia said. "You were damned fast."

"Why the rush? Even we haven't swam this far out." Rosie said.

Sarina smiled like a child who had just been pumped with candies.

"Yeah. You know, I could swim fast, faster than normal people even before I became a mermaid. Now, with the tail, I can swim super fast. It was so exhilarating…"

Sarina went on with her effusion. She did not notice Rosie and Olivia's eyes staring fixated past her, with their lips slightly parted.

"…I felt like I could go faster if I wanted. It was just there, the strength, the energy, I could feel it bubbling underneath. It was there for me. Do you… get me?"

Sarina seemed to come down from the peak of rhapsody, when

51

she noticed that she had been soaring all alone. She looked at her cousins, and only just then, did she see the look on their faces. Their eyes were fixed, staring straight through her. Staring at something…

Sarina turned, and then her heart pounded.

Not too far away from where they floated, was a sight they did not expect to see. A merman. A strange merman.

The merman's face was a palette of shock and surprise. In all his life in the sea, he had never seen any other mermaid. Not even a woman. Like the one he saw right now. He was riveted, transfixed by her beauty. Her body full of curves. Her eyes were almond-shaped, and brown, coffee brown. He noticed how her hair, was blue, a darker shade than the sea, ran in smooth streams, falling below her shoulders. Suddenly, a hand clasped her shoulder, and he noticed the other mermaids flanking her sides, making them three in total. They too, were beautiful visions. But the mermaid with the blue hair seemed to draw him in. There was something about her.

Sarina felt like she was plunging into something, something she had no control over. Her eyes ran over the strange merman in the water. A strong muscular torso, long blonde hair, stopping just at the nape of his neck, large captivating eyes. She was enamoured. She had never seen a merman before. And she was thrilled. She thought he was the most beautiful man she had ever seen.

Suddenly, a sharp whisper, went into her ear, like a bullet, startling her from her daydream. She turned. Rosie and Olivia's eyes were balls of alarm.

"What's the problem?" Sarina asked, her voice on a low tone.

"I think we should go", Rosie said.

"What? Why?" Sarina asked, flinging her eyes towards the man, who still bobbed afar off in the water, casting uncertain looks at them.

"This is important and urgent. We should go." Rosie whispered sharply.

"That may be one of the harp guards we told you about," Olivia said, sending cautious looks at the man.

"But you said you saw them at the Long Room, and that they followed you home from Dublin. I didn't see anything. No one followed me." Sarina protested.

"That's it," Olivia said sharply. "That's it. Isn't it odd, that Rosie was followed, or that the guards were everywhere when Elan and I went there, but nothing for you? Think about this, Sarina. It may have been a trap. An elaborate scheme created to make us lower our guard, to be less suspicious when they swoop in. That," she held herself from pointing at the man, "is swooping in."

Sarina took one more look at the man. Her eyes shone with reluctance. But Rosie and Olivia were right.

She looked back at Olivia, who was piercing her with an urgent gaze.

"I suggest that we split up. In doing so, we split his attention, and we get away easily." Olivia said, flashing Rosie and Sarina a questioning look.

They both nodded their understanding.

They turned, and diving into the water, sped away in different directions.

"Wait", the man yelled, lurching forward.

He stopped. A cloud of disappointment settled on his face. His lips opened and closed, like they wanted to say something. There was a persistent tug inside him, a nagging. He wanted to follow them. The blue-haired girl especially. And he didn't know why.

His vision was sharp enough, so he could see her, the girl with the blue hair, growing small in the distance. He noticed, how fiercely the sea rippled around her. His eyes increased, his forehead wrinkled. The girl, she was fast. Very fast. Faster than anything on the sea should be. A smile broke out on his face, like sweat on a skin surface. She had the powers of speed. The same as him.

9

Sarina could feel that pool of energy bubbling within. Though she was new to the feel of it, she had already come to cherish it. The surface of the water broke, forming little walls that flanked Sarina as she sped through. She could feel the pricks of urgency within her, stimulating her to go faster and faster. She had no way of knowing where Olivia and Rosie were. But she was certain they would meet at the beach, or at most at the cottage.

She looked behind her and had almost taken her face away, when she took her face back in alarm.

Swimming behind her, and coming up at an alarming rate, was the merman. The one they had just fled from. Sarina turned and willed herself to go faster. She zipped through the water now, an inch or two below its surface.

She looked back again. He was closer than before. Her

mind was a chaos of thoughts, her heartbeat out of tempo.

Sarina stopped just in time to avoid colliding into a cliff wall, rising above the surface. Water splashed on her tail, forming a spread like peacock feathers. She turned and pressed herself further into the wall. It was cold, and rough, and hard.

The merman stopped a few feet from her.

He stared at her. She stared back.

Sarina's heart was marathon racing. The merman's face was a mould of uncertainty. It was as though he were about to explore uncharted waters.

"Hello", he greeted, his voice, a smooth baritone, travelled across to Sarina.

Sarina's lips quivered. Her heart leapt, when she noticed the merman edging closer. She had no way of escape. Her vision began to blur as a film of tears grew over it. She dug her chin into her shoulder and cried. Cried, because she had just begun to enjoy the magic and fantasy of being a mermaid. Cried because she was about to lose it all due to a harp guard.

The merman edged closer and closer, his eyes focused intently on Sarina.

Suddenly, Sarina spread her arms out towards him.

"Please." She cried. "Please don't kill me."

The merman froze. A stunned look, falling over his face like a blindfold.

"Kill you?" he asked, after a few moments, where the swish of waves sounded against the cliff wall, and Sarina's sobs were all that pervaded the awkwardness surrounding them both.

The merman lifted his hands, very slowly, out of the water.

"Here", he said, his voice as gentle as the feel of a feather.

"Here", he said again, showing Sarina that his hands were empty.

Sarina still churned out fear like wisps of radiation from a ball of gas.

"Please don't kill me", she said again, this time her voice was barely a whisper.

A look of frustration flashed on the merman's face. His voice rose an octave.

"Kill you? Why would I do that?" he asked, spreading his arms out. "I've lived most of my life in solitude. I did not know mermaids exist… Why would I kill the first mermaid I've ever met?"

There was something about his voice, the shrill tone of urgency and passion in it, that made her lower her arms. And her heart slow to a trot. She looked into his eyes, and they engaged her. Those pools of greenish-blue held her transfixed. Then she blinked, a voice in the back of her mind reminding her that this could be a scheme by the harp guards to get at her. The distrust that was sluicing off her, flowed back in, gathering into a firm pool.

Sarina's mind spun, trying to take in the scenario, evaluating, calculating. Suddenly she saw an opening between her and the merman. She lurched forward with urgency.

The man had seen the mermaid's eyes flick left and right. As though she searched desperately for something. Just then, he saw her look beside him, and in the spur of the moment, he realised what was about to happen. He moved, adjusting his body, as he saw her speed to his left.

Sarina had sped past the man by a hair's breadth, when she felt something wrap around her wrists, stopping her dead in the water.

She turned, her heart beating like a rattle. She flashed a

look at her wrists, but warm fingers wrapped gently around them holding her back. The man was careful to apply just as much strength and gentility to his grip as would restrain Sarina from leaving without hurting her.

"Stay for a moment. Please." He said.

There was something in his voice, a softness, and a fierceness of emotion, which perfused Sarina like water to foam. She found the tautness in her ebbing. She looked at him.

"Please tell me your name." The merman said. "Your name, that's all. And I'll let you go."

Sarina looked at him. There it was again. That sincerity, and passion in his voice. It was gentle, yet heated. Very capable of stirring unexpected emotions.

"I'm Kyan." He said, piercing her with eyes that sent her heart racing.

"Sarina", she replied, her voice a whisper.

The man watched her speed away, the surface of the water breaking into low walls beside her. His lips parted. And hung there for a moment.

Then he whispered.

"My pearl."

He sank into the water, and sped away, through an incoming wave, and out to sea.

10

Rosie and Olivia stood at the edge of the beach, waves from the sea licking their feet, and stared out into the sea. For the umpteenth time.

"Ugh", Rosie groaned and stomped a few feet away from the lip of the beach.

Olivia was panicking.

"She should be here." She said. Uncertainty creeping into her voice.

"Right?" Rosie said, concern whittling her voice into a scream. "With her speed, one would think that she would get here before us."

"I think we should go look for her," Olivia said.

"Yeah? I've only suggested that to you like a thousand times." Rosie said.

"Come on, Rosie. This is no time for quips. Plus, how was I

supposed to know that she would take this long to arrive?"

Rosie heaved a sigh, and walked back to the edge of the water, stepping in beside Olivia.

"Let's go get her," Olivia said, her voice carrying the tone of finality.

She began to step further into the water, when…

"Look!" Rosie shouted.

Olivia turned towards Rosie and noticed her hand pointing further into the sea. She turned and saw the surface of the water break into a moving furrow. The furrow came closer and closer, until the body of something began to emerge from the water.

Rosie blinked and slouched as she exhaled with relief. Olivia's face which was heavy with concern and worry moments ago, was bleached. The slight hue of joy sat in its place.

Sarina walked out of the water and onto the beach. Water dripped off her hair, down to her body, and pattered to the ground.

"Sarina", Rosie called, rushing in towards her.

Olivia moved closer to Sarina.

Sarina saw the relief on the girl's faces and felt a surge of guilt from inside her.

"I'm so sorry, girls", she said before any of them could open their mouths. She held their gaze imploringly.

"So, so sorry." She added.

"Hell, Sarina. Where have you been?" Rosie asked.

"Something happened," Sarina said.

"Something happened?" Olivia asked. "We were worried about you."

"Yeah, I know. And I said I'm sorry." Sarina whined.

Rosie and Olivia were silent.

"Besides, it's not really my fault. I'm not familiar with these waters. And since we split, I got a little confused on the way."

Rosie *hmm*-ed.

"Yeah, that's true. We're sorry." Olivia said. "But given the circumstances, we couldn't think of anything better. Finally, you're safe. We shook off the guard."

"Yeah", Sarina said, drawing out her speech, "about that." She winced.

The shadow of alarm crossed the sister's faces.

"Sarina," Olivia called. "What is it?"

Sarina flicked her eyes to Rosie, whose eyes were wells of expectation, and back to Olivia.

"This is better said inside," Sarina said, heaving a sigh.

Olivia pursed her lips.

"Come on", Sarina said, tugging at Olivia's arm. Then she flung her eyes to Rosie. "I promise, we'll talk about this when we get in."

Rosie replied with an "mm" and a furrow of her brow.

They turned and walked off the beach. Water flowed down their hair in little rivulets and melded into their swimsuits. The tide from the sea licked the edge of the shore, washing away the footprints left behind by the girls.

11

Rosie came down the stairs to the living room and picked up an old book from the shelf. She settled into an armchair, and flipped through the musty pages, while she waited for Olivia and Sarina.

While skimming through the words in the book, she heard the hum of an engine stop, just somewhere around the house. Most probably, the parking lot out the back.

She heard the thud of footsteps out on the porch, then a knock on the door.

"Who's there?" Rosie called.

"It's me." said a shrill voice.

A smile spread on Rosie's face.

"You can come in, Nessa, it's open" She called out.

The door creaked as it opened. Vanessa stood at the doorway, a lidded basket in her hand, and a profuse smile on her face.

"Won't you come say hi?" she asked.

Rosie beamed. She stood up from the chair and walked into Vanessa's open arms.

Vanessa *mm*-ed, relishing the embrace.

"I've really missed you," Rosie said, before breaking out the embrace.

"And I've missed you, Rosie," Vanessa said, taking Rosie in with eyes slathered with affection. "But I'm here now."

She moved in, past Rosie, and dropping the basket on the coffee table, fell into a couch.

Rosie shut the door, and settling back into the armchair, flung the old book on the table.

"What were you reading?" Vanessa asked, picking the book up.

"Nothing particularly fascinating. It's just an old narrative woven around the defeat of the Spanish Armada during the reign of Elizabeth I."

Vanessa wrinkled her nose.

"Sounds boring to me." She said, dropping the book with a loud thud on the table.

Just then Olivia and Sarina walked into the living room, almost simultaneously.

"Nessa", Olivia crooned.

Vanessa smiled. She stood from the couch, and hugged Olivia. Then she looked at Sarina and smiled.

"Sarina", Vanessa said, spreading her arms.

Sarina went into the embrace with a pleasant "mm".

They soon settled to a meal of pleasant chatter. And after a while, took the talking, and a tray of coffee, to the porch.

"Yeah", Vanessa said, drawing attention to herself. "So I brought some goodies. A little something to whet your tongues."

She turned the lid to the basket over.

Sarina squealed with delight.

"Oh yeah, baby," Vanessa said with excitement and a tinge of pride. "Just for your information, it is important that you know that these chocolate croissants were made by yours truly."

Sarina took one of the croissants, her fingers sinking into the melting chocolate. Then she bit into it, taking in some of the warm sweet chocolate.

"Hmm. This is so nice." She said.

"Thank you Sarina", Vanessa fawned.

As they ate and drank, they talked, weaving in and out of topics, till they steered into their swim earlier in the day. And their encounter with the strange merman. Rosie narrated the story, while Vanessa listened with characteristic raptness. Then she cued in Sarina to fulfil her promise. And also because fulfilling her promise, continued the rest of their story.

Sarina wiped her hands on a napkin, then she dropped her almost empty cup of coffee on the tray beside her. She sat up, and leaned with her elbows on the left arm of her chair.

"Well", she began, "we had split. You know, to lose the merman. I used my powers."

"Powers?" Vanessa asked, her face, a blossom of surprise. She had been filled in on Sarina being a mermaid, but knew nothing of her powers.

"Yeah", Rosie jumped in, "Sarina's got speed."

"Speed?" Vanessa asked. "Is that a thing? I thought you were all fast?"

"Yeah. But she's super fast. You should see her."

"Cool," Vanessa said, a glow of admiration kindling on her face.

"Yeah", Sarina said, "so I sped off. I wasn't familiar with the water. I'm still not familiar with it. So, the goal at the time was just to go as far away from him as possible, and in the process find my way back to shore." She flung her eyes from Olivia, to Rosie, to Vanessa. Holding their gazes and making sure she had their attention. She did.

"He followed me." She blurted.

It took moments for it to register. But they got it. Olivia's face was the first to bloom with comprehension.

"He followed you", she whispered.

"Yeah, he did," Sarina replied matter-of-factly.

"So, he caught up with you?" Rosie asked. It was not really a question. It was more like a statement.

"Yeah, he did. The cliff wall I nearly ran into in my state of panic, helped in slowing me down."

They all looked at Sarina. Their eyes bearing the marks of an unspoken question. The impact of their gaze on her began to make her skin tingle uncomfortably.

"Okay, okay", she said, the words bursting out her mouth.

"We talked."

"You talked?" Rosie asked incredulously.

"Not talk, like talk. It was more like, he insisted we at least introduce ourselves."

"Sarina." Olivia cried. "Just what were you thinking? It's no ordinary thing that you're here now. Alive. Saving your life was the reason why we fled in the first place."

"I know. I know." Sarina replied, flinging her eyes around. Anywhere, but into the accusatory looks the girls wore.

"Look", she said, "just hear me out. I didn't stop for a friendly talk. I was cornered. I even tried speeding past him. But guess what? He stopped me!"

The looks of blame bled out the girls' faces. They had seen the fervency with which Sarina tried to convey the actuality of what transpired. They looked at each other uneasily.

"Kept me from going." Sarina continued. "Because he was just as fast."

She stopped now to breathe. She flung her eyes towards the ceiling, trying to curtail the first signs of tears from building into a stream.

"Uhm… Sarina", Olivia called. Her voice, a bit tremulous.

There was no reply.

Olivia forged on anyway.

"We just want to say we're sorry."

"Yes, yes we are." Rosie and Vanessa said, in an unorderly chorus.

"We're just looking out for you, that's all. We've had encounters with these guys. We know their directives. They're merciless."

"If Adian were here, he would tell you more," Vanessa said.

Sarina sighed and spoke after a short spell of silence.

"I understand. And I'm grateful, very grateful that you all look out for my safety. But he wasn't."

"Wasn't what?" Vanessa asked.

"A harp guard," Sarina replied.

There was a bout of silence.

Olivia was the first to break it.

"How sure are you about this?" she asked.

"He's lived in solitude and has never seen a mermaid. Thought they didn't exist. We're the first he's seeing." Sarina said.

"He told you this himself?" Rosie asked.

"Yes," Sarina replied. "He didn't want to hurt me."

"Yeah?" Vanessa said. "Then why'd he stop you?"

"To ask for my name," Sarina replied.

The girls flashed themselves looks that were latent with alarm.

"And to tell me his," Sarina added.

"He told you his name?" Rosie asked, her eyes perking up in surprise.

"Yeah."

Vanessa flicked her eyes wide, gesturing for Sarina to be more forthcoming.

"Kyan… Kyan is his name."

Silence wrapped itself comfortably around the girls for a while. Till Rosie shook it off.

"Well", she said, "now that we have a name, it'll be easier to track him, or to learn more about him."

"Or not," Vanessa interjected.

Rosie gave her a questioning look.

Vanessa sighed.

"You're forgetting something." She said. "If the merman has been solitary most of his life, like he says, there won't be anything to find out."

"Yeah. Yeah." Rosie said, nodding, as the truth of what Vanessa said sank in.

Olivia nodded too.

"However", Sarina chipped in, her voice a bit cheerier than before, "we can still ask the boys when they get back."

"Yes", Olivia said. "We'll ask Elan and Adian if he is a guard or a protector. And Ervin, if he recognizes Kyan as a fellow merman from the sea."

The girls nodded, or murmured their consent.

That settled, they gradually picked up a new conversation, reviving the cheery mood among themselves. And descended into a two-in-one course of yammering, and laughter.

12

The next morning saw a sky – a beautiful mix of azure on pillow-*y* whites – and the trio of Rosie, Olivia, and Sarina, having breakfast at Vanessa's café. Breakfast was pancakes – nice and thin – served with lemon juice.

"How's preparation for the wedding?" Vanessa asked in between sips of her tea.

Olivia's eyelids fluttered, as a smile broke on her face.

"Show off", Rosie joked.

They all laughed.

"Well, the boys aren't back from their tour of the Pacific yet," Olivia said.

"They must be having some sort of bachelor party down there," Sarina said.

"Yeah. I bet you they are." Rosie said.

"All that blue. Their scouring the bottom of the Pacific. It's the dream." Sarina said, the glamour of a daydream settling on her face like dew.

"Yeah. I reckon." Vanessa said, a dull look enveloping her face.

Rosie gave Vanessa an affectionate look. Olivia shared it too. Vanessa was the odd one among the four of them. She shared a love for the sea, almost as ferocious as theirs. But she couldn't tour the sea, as she would want to. The three of them – Rosie, Olivia, and most recently, Sarina – were epitomes of things she fiercely desired, but she felt she could never get.

"Nessa", Rosie called dotingly. She stretched her hand and clamped it affectionately on Vanessa's wrist.

"It's no problem," Vanessa said, sitting up, and shaking off the dullness from her face.

Rosie squeezed gently, then let go of Vanessa's wrist.

"So what new plans have you set in place for the wedding?" Vanessa asked, her voice taking on an inflection of cheeriness. It was almost as if the gloom she wore moments ago had been a spectre. "I know I'm still in charge of the cake, and Cara the cooking."

"There's no question about that." Olivia fawned. "Well, I've finally come up with a venue. Or an idea for a venue. Seeing as Ervin's not here, and his opinion hasn't been sought."

"Spill it out already," Vanessa said, too eagerly.

Olivia flashed a look Rosie's way.

"The beach." She spat.

Sarina flung her eyes from Olivia, to Rosie, and then let them settle on Vanessa. She was trying to gauge her reaction.

Before now, Rosie and Olivia had had a little dispute over the wedding venue. A dispute Sarina had opted to absolve herself from.

Now she wanted to hear what Vanessa would put in.

"Oh, my God", Vanessa droned, her eyes, organic flames of awe. "You're not kidding, are you?" she asked.

"Not in the slightest", Olivia said, the suspicion of a smile on her face.

"It's brilliant," Vanessa said, her voice heightened with excitement. "Straight-out-of-the-skies brilliant." She gushed.

Olivia's lips spread, revealing teeth glowing with satisfaction. She sent Rosie a winning look. Rosie rolled her eyes to the side. Sarina smiled.

"You can't really be serious," Rosie said to Vanessa. "Ugh", she groaned.

"What? What's the problem?" Vanessa asked. Her eyes jumping from one girl to the other.

Rosie was mildly put off. Olivia was smiling self-satisfactorily. Sarina was... Well, Sarina was the only one who seemed unaffected.

"Tell me what the problem is, Sarina?" Vanessa asked, looking expectantly at her.

Sarina flashed her cousins a look, then looked at Vanessa.

"Back at the cottage, before we came here," she began, "Olivia, well, got an idea for a venue. The beach, like she just said. But Rosie disagreed with it…"

"I still disagree with it." Rosie interrupted, then leaned into her seat, sulking mildly.

Sarina nodded. Vanessa gestured for her to go on.

"Well, there you have it. She still disagrees." Sarina said conclusively.

"That's it?" Vanessa asked, a bit taken aback.

"Uhm, yeah," Sarina said. Her eyes flashed with uncertainty. She was unsure of where Vanessa was really going.

"I mean", Vanessa said, "there has to be a reason." Her statement, was toned to sound more like a question.

Sarina looked at Rosie. Trying to get her to reply. Rosie was still sulking.

"I think she wanted the wedding to hold at the town hall. That way, she said, they could account for the people that came in, thereby ensuring our safety," Sarina said.

"Aaaaawn", Vanessa cooed, flashing Rosie eyes mildewed with adoration. "That's cute."

"Exactly what I told her," Olivia said, sitting up. "I told her it was really nice and thoughtful of her. But come on you all, it's my wedding. And though I don't want to subject us to the danger of being in the open, but we do go out in the open every day, don't we?"

"Yeah", Rosie said matter-of-factly, "but not when there's going to be a little crowd which would prove excellent foliage for hiding."

She lapsed back into her chair.

Silence had them all in a vice-like grip. But only for a few moments.

"Okay", Olivia said, sitting up, and placing her arms on the table. She looked imploringly at Rosie. "Here goes. I really want this wedding to be on the beach. I want to have the moments etched memorably in my mind. The crashing of the waves and the tweets of the birds on the surrounding hillside, serenading our vows. The sea breeze, cool and soft, causing my gown to billow, my veil to dance. The scent of flowers wrapping everywhere in a loving embrace."

Vanessa and Sarina's demeanour softened. Even, Rosie, who up till a moment ago was sulking, listened with enamoured interest.

"It's the dream, girls. The dream. And", she looked at Rosie now, and placed a hand on hers, "because I don't want to do anything without Rosie's consent. I'll let you plan the wedding.

You know create the parameters for the invitation, the section of the beach to be used, and all that."

Vanessa reached for a handkerchief and dabbed at the edges of her eyes. Sarina bent her head to the side, and looked at the scene with eyes glistening with admiration.

Even a heart made of solid rock would split under this shower of emotion. How much more Rosie's. She turned and looked at Olivia, her eyes softening, like melting butter, into pools of affection.

"I was just being concerned. For you. For all of us." She said.

"I know," Olivia replied.

"Well, since I'm planning your wedding, I'll make it more memorable. I promise." She said, her face shining with truth, and a smile.

Olivia smiled in return.

"Okay", Vanessa said, sniffing, "now that you both are done bringing tears to our eyes. Can we go do something else, please? Time's flying."

They laughed.

The girls – Sarina, Rosie, Olivia – bid Vanessa goodbye, after a short session of teasing Vanessa about Adian.

They walked down the cobbled path abutting the café. Then they took a bend to the left, and Rosie's shop came into view.

They stood for some seconds as Rosie opened the padlock holding the gate of corrugated metal. She lifted the gate upwards, and it made a grating sound as it receded into its space on the post. She slid a key into the keyhole of the main doors made of glass, then she pushed and they swerved in.

Sarina sighed. She had been in Rosie's shop once or twice. Yet, she still felt that surge of awe, as fresh as she would feel if she was seeing it for the first time. There was an array of shelves neatly arranged like a stack of cards, in rows and columns. And a company of shells, beauties from the sea, unique and rare, lined these shelves. The shells, a burst of colours, against the brown of the shelves, was a sweet mix, impressing on the eyes, a vision of lustre. Further down, there were rectangular recesses in the wall, in which necklaces, made from seashells, hung on little hooks. Each of the recesses were covered by screens of glass, that could slide open and close. The necklaces possessed an organic beauty. There glitter, not as sparkly as gold, but glittery all the same, arrested the eye and the heart.

Besides the shell shop, was a screened off bay, still in the same building, where Rosie read angel and tarot cards to interested customers.

Just then, the entry bell chimed. They all turned to see a young girl with caramel-coloured hair let the door slide close behind her.

"Wow, hello." The girl said. "You're early."

"Morning, Miriam. I have someplace to be, so I decided to open early. This is my cousin Sarina by the way"

Miriam turned to Sarina and Olivia. Rosie had employed her as a shop assistant, a few weeks into the establishment of her shell business.

"Hello Sarina, Olivia", she greeted.

"Hello." Olivia and Sarina echoed alternately.

"Okay", Rosie said with a sigh. Her eyes went to her wristwatch. "I think Cliffside should be well awake by now. And the customers will be here anytime soon." She looked at Sarina. "I was supposed to accompany Olivia to make wedding arrangements. But with my newly elevated position, I will be doing more than that. So, over to you, Sarina." She turned to Miriam. "Miriam, you'll be working with Sarina today, okay?"

Miriam smiled and nodded. Then proceeded behind the counter.

Sarina gushed with smiles, as Rosie and Olivia walked toward the door.

"I won't chase away your customers." She called from behind them.

Rosie turned her head a little to the side, still walking. "I trust you not to." She called in return.

Olivia laughed.

Rosie stopped by the door, to flick the close-open sign. Then she walked out.

Anyone walking down the street would see the sign with 'OPEN' in bold white letters against a turquoise placard, glaring through the glass doors.

13

osie's shop had become the mitochondrion of Cliffside. Customers trooped in and trooped out. Miriam would smile at the counter, and with a flick of her hand direct the customers further down the short aisle that led from the door, where they would meet Sarina. Sarina would help them through the shelves of shells and necklaces. On seeing the shells and the necklaces, the customers all registered the same expression. That of awe. Of wonder. Sarina would entertain the resulting effusion, and prune their spontaneous desires towards purchasing a particular shell or necklace. Being surrounded by the treasures of the sea that Rosie had collected thrilled her.

Soon, there was an intermission in the flow of customers. Miriam slouched a bit in her chair behind the counter and clicked away on her phone.

Sarina sat on a stool, just at the tip of one of the shelf passageways. And then from thinking of the elation she felt from seeing the awe on the customer's faces leaving the store after having made purchases, she lapsed into a panorama of memories.

Ultimately, Sarina found a stop along the track of her memories. The trail of a smile painted her face, giving it a degree of smugness. Her mind was replete with thoughts of having a merman protector, just like her cousins had. Just like Vanessa had. And then the projections followed. Creations, images, that reshaped themselves amorphously, as she added and removes features that would belong to her protector.

"Will he be tall?" She thought. "Muscular? Thin." "Or would he just be like…"

The image of Kyan, the merman she had seen from the day before, the only merman she had seen, popped into her mind. And then like a magnet, engaged all the tentacles of her mind. She saw his eyes, greenish-blue eyes that gave off a liquid quality. Much like the shimmering of the sea. His masculine strong chiselled looks. She felt a thrill run through her heart. Then she painted Kyan as her protector. For a time, it was roses and sunshine, till an image, prickly like a thorn, obtruded her daydream. It was the image of him, seeing them, with shock written in bold fonts on his face.

"He wouldn't be shocked if he were my protector." Rosie thought with uncertainty. "No, he wouldn't. He was seeing us for the first time."

The thought, the truth of its conclusion, pulled her spirits down a bit.

Then she remembered Rosie and Olivia speaking, saying something about the protector following from Dublin.

The thought, that a merman out there had followed her from the library filled her with mortification, as she thought well about it. Whoever it was, she thought, may have seen her episode – where she yelled and stormed out on her cheating boyfriend trudging her suitcase along with her.

Suddenly, as if from another world, she heard a jingle. The sound jerked her from her reverie, to see a young man walk in through the door. He was tall. Very tall. And thin. On a strange impulse, Sarina got up and looked over at the man.

"Hi", she greeted, a pleasant smile creamed on her face.

The man flung his eyes across the array of shelves as though he was not certain of how to go about inspecting them for purchase.

"Just looking." The man said turning away, when he spotted Miriam.

Just then the entry bell dinged. And another man came through the door. Sarina flung her eyes towards the new man. The new man was tall as well. Spikes of excitement went through Sarina's heart, as she took in the physique of the new man. He was fit and muscular. His T-shirt clung neatly to his body, the sleeves wrapped around his muscled arms.

"He may be my protector. Or one of them is." Sarina thought.

The men walked around the shop, their eyes scaling the items on the shelves, and in the cases that receded into the walls. Their eyes seemed to connect with one another's at intervals during their walk around the shop.

The first man that had walked into the shop, walked out without a word. The door had not closed behind him, when the second man, the muscly one, followed suit.

Halfway through the door, he paused. Then he turned and flashed Sarina a cheeky smile. Sarina's heart gave a solid thump, then subsided like a wave. Then he walked out the door.

Sarina's heart was fluttering. Her palms were sweating softly.

"He has to be my protector." She thought. "He has to be. He is."

She flashed Miriam a look. She was busy behind the counter, scribbling something on paper. Sarina moved backwards into the company of shelves and began to do a little dance, fueled by an immeasurable surge of happiness.

Sarina was deeply immersed in her little celebration. She did not see the duo that just walked through the door. And were walking towards her, looks of amused curiosity decking their faces like powder.

14

Rosie and Olivia walked slowly. They were talking, their faces, plaques of semi-seriousness, their hands, making gestures in the air. The arrangements they had gone out to make for the wedding had been successful. Everything had been just as they expected.

The duo stopped talking, as soon as they came to the door of the shop, Rosie's shop. Then Rosie pushed open the door and went in, Olivia following closely.

The entry bell dinged, causing Miriam to look up from her work. She smiled.

"Hi, Rosie." She greeted. "Is this welcome?" she asked.

Rosie smiled.

"Yup. You can say that." She replied, her eyes focused straight ahead, as it had picked up something in its sights.

"Just what has our cousin been up to?" Olivia asked, her eyes picking up the same thing Rosie's had.

They looked at Sarina and amusement, kindled with curiosity, enveloped them.

"Why don't we go find out," Rosie said, already moving towards Sarina.

Sarina was still dancing, like a ballerina without a ball, when she was interrupted by a voice.

"Care to fill us in on what's happening?"

She turned abruptly, a bit startled.

"Hey guys", she greeted, recognition dawning on her face like a splash of water.

"Hey," Rosie replied.

"Come on", Olivia pressed. "What's the acrobatics for?"

"Obviously a celebration's in order." Rosie jested.

"Do we bring a bottle of wine? We could go to the pub, you know. Or just go to Vanessa's. Or better still Cara's. That'll be the best." Olivia said.

Rosie hummed and nodded her assent.

"Come on guys", Sarina said, then giggled. "It's really no big deal." She said, with exaggerated disinterest.

"You bet," Rosie said.

They waited. Leaned softly on the side of the shelves, and

folded their arms, boring through Sarina with the expectancy in their eyes.

"Okay", Sarina said, as though she had been caught red-handed. "It is a big deal."

"Yeah," Olivia said. And smiled.

"Now we get to know what we're celebrating about," Rosie added.

Sarina took the both of them in, her face, a non-expendable fountain of smiles. Then she moved in towards them.

"They are here." She said in a conspiratorial whisper. "They must have followed me."

Her face spread to accommodate a smug smile.

On the other hand, Rosie and Olivia were taken aback. The shadow of confusion settled over them.

"Who is here?" Rosie asked.

"Who followed you?" Olivia asked.

Their eyes lay on Sarina with a smouldering intensity. They were confused. And were even more, with her flagrant display of excitement.

"Spit it out already please, Sarina," Rosie said, her voice hushed with urgency.

"My protectors. They walked into the shop earlier. In fact, you'd just missed them." She said.

Olivia and Rosie looked at each other.

"What protectors?" Olivia asked.

Sarina looked at them, puzzled for a moment. Then a smile broke out, like rays of the sun piercing through a thick foliage of clouds.

"Oh. I see what you're doing." She said.

"What are we doing, Sarina," Rosie said, flashing Olivia a look laden with hidden meaning.

"Come on," Sarina said, flinging her arms into the air, and letting them fall with a slap to the sides of her body. "Protectors. I mean you two have them. Vanessa does. You said they would follow me from Dublin, to protect me from the harp guards who may want to kill me."

Rosie oh-ed, and flashed Olivia another look. There was the obvious suspicion of suppressed reservations lurking behind their eyes.

"So", Olivia said, blinking herself out from a torrent of assailing thoughts, "you said they."

"Yeah, two tall, good –looking men," Sarina said.

"Okay. So they're tall and good-looking, alright. That means they're your protectors?" Rosie asked.

"I don't know. I felt so." She said.

"And the two of them are your protectors," Olivia said. Her

statement sounded more like a question.

"Right?" Sarina asked, with glee in her eyes.

"Come on", she said, caving under the looks of incredulity her cousins sent her way. "I was just joking. Surely, it has to be one of them."

"Yeah. Yeah. Absolutely." Olivia said, nodding her head exaggeratedly.

She stabbed a thought through to Rosie's mind,

"We'll have concrete answers, and a better resolution to this, when the boys get back."

Rosie blinked her assent.

They spoke some more. Dove into light details of Sarina's experience in the shop, and the proceedings for the wedding arrangements. Then Sarina said she was heading back to the cottage.

The sisters watched her walk out the door, flouncing.

Then they stared into each other's eyes, sharing the clouds of worry that hovered in their eyes, and shining from behind all that, a determination, an unspoken course of action as they hurriedly rushed after Sarina.

Protect Sarina. At all costs.

15

T hey're here." Olivia said. Her voice was squealy, barely able to contain the tremors of excitement running through her.

"What?" Vanessa said, sitting up abruptly.

They were out at the beach, bathing in the soft rays of the evening sun, as it traced a receding path down the sky. They – Olivia, Rosie, Vanessa, and Sarina – sat, spaced on mats.

"How'd you know that?" Sarina asked.

"You forget she reads minds, eh?" Vanessa chipped in.

Sarina oh-ed.

She had been intimidated by their powers. But since they weren't as physical and superficial as hers, it was relatively easy to forget about them. She looked at Olivia and noticed that she had a distant look in her eyes. Like she was poking the skirts, of where the sea met with the horizon, trying to see beyond that straight line.

"They're a few leagues out. But they've entered familiar waters." Olivia said.

She *hmm* -ed, and lay back a little.

She could not have accessed the location of the boys if Ervin were not there. The strengths of her power being limited by proximity. She communicated with him through their special bond. A two-way telepathic connection enabled Ervin to speak back to her; and that was because Ervin had telepathic powers, although of a lesser degree. His only worked with sea animals. For the rest, it was just plain mind-reading, as with others. She could plant a thought in their minds, but that was it.

Her heart waltzed with excitement. She could not believe she had missed Ervin this much. She was sure the other girls felt the same too. She looked at them, then thought,

"The other girls apart from Sarina."

Her mood was clouded by a thin haze of hurt, and empathy.

When Sarina had told her of her boyfriend's infidelity, more than anything, Olivia had felt a stab of anger. If she had seen him, there and then, she would have given him a furious talk.

"Men suck." She thought. "Well, not all of them."

She looked at Sarina again. She was saying something to Vanessa, and smiling radiantly. Olivia was struck by the display of rural simplicity Sarina exuded. Now, they had to protect her. From giving herself over too eagerly into another romantic affair. And she was on a quick flight to doing just that.

Just then, a thought dropped into her mind.

"We're here."

It was Ervin.

She sat up and stretched her eyes towards the sea. She saw something on the water. Using her hands, she lifted herself off the mat. On her feet, she could see better.

There were ripples at the surface of the sea, snaking in towards land.

She did not need to speak. The girls had noticed her renewed interest in the sea and jumped to their feet.

They saw the ripples. The trails of violent effervescence, leaving behind plumes of surf. All of them flung their eyes out, their hearts dancing to expectant tunes. The looks of longing and excitement mushroomed on their faces.

Sarina exuded excitement. Kyan was the only merman she had seen. These would be the second. And they were friends. Family.

She saw their heads jut out the water. Three in number. Then the rest of their body followed. It was as though they grew, steadily, from the belly of the river. Olivia had adapted the men's swimsuits as well as hers and Rosie's.

Sarina's lips parted slightly, creating a little line- *y* space, which birthed an inaudible gasp. She was taken, swept off her feet, by the sight of the men coming out the sea. Rivulets of water dripped from their hair and slithered down their bare strong upper bodies. The cascading wetness gave their pristinely carved muscles an audible pizzazz. One of them was a few inches shy of meeting up to the height of his confreres. He had short dark hair, matted to the sides of his head. The other two had shoulder-length dark hair tied into ponytails. One thing they shared in common, apart from the good looks, and the razzmatazz of their entrance, was the smiles on their faces. Effulgent. Like the smile of a new moon on the dark azure of the night sky. And laden with excitement.

Suddenly, squeals and whoops split the evening air. Sarina turned just in time to see the girls run off towards the men. She felt sharp spikes of ambivalence. A part of her wanted to centrifuge. To run along with the girls.

"But to meet whom." She thought.

This was the first time she was meeting any of the mermen. She felt a cold splash of awkwardness at the prospect of jumping into an embrace with them. So she stayed put. Uncertain. And a bit queasy.

The girls flung themselves into the arms of their men, regardless of their wet bodies. It was a beautiful sight. The reunion of a troika of lovebirds. Ervin clasped his arms around the small of Olivia's back and twirled with her.

"Did you miss me?" he asked when he finally set her down.

Olivia looked into his eyes, warm pools of unbridled love. Her cheeks flushed.

"You wish." She said, blinking and looking away from him.

"Hello, beautiful." Elan greeted.

"Hello, handsome," Rosie said, smiling.

"That's it?" he asked, feigning surprise. "No more words? I mean I leave you for such a length of time, and 'hello handsome' is all you can say?"

"Don't you even start," Rosie said, affecting a sulky face.

"Oh come here," Elan said, opening his arms again, inviting her for a second embrace.

Rosie accepted the invitation, nestling her head into the solidity of his throbbing chest. This second embrace was gentle, lacking the bustle of the previous one, and more intimate. When finally they broke up, it was too stare into each other's eyes, and pass emotions that were too potent to take the form of words.

Suddenly, and with surprising speed, Elan scooped Rosie up from the ground. Her mouth spurted a scream that soon melded into laughter.

Adian and Vanessa shared a long passionate kiss. They broke off and stayed apart for a bit, their lips slightly parted, hanging in tight proximity. Their lips met again, in a short perky embrace, and then they looked into each other's eyes.

"Shouldn't we go in?" Olivia asked aloud.

They all chorused a yes, or hummed their affirmation.

"I wish I was a mermaid," Vanessa grumbled, giving Adian a nudge with the blade of her shoulder.

They all laughed.

Sarina moved forward to meet them as they walked up.

"Hey, Sarina." Ervin greeted, a smile on his face.

Sarina was a bit taken aback. She had not told him his name. As if he had read and comprehended the look on her face, Ervin said,

"Ah. Don't mind me. Olivia here, had just told me your name." He made a pointing gesture towards the side of his head. "With her mind."

Sarina smiled.

"Pleased to meet you,…" she dipped her head, making an expectant gesture.

"Ervin. The name's Ervin." He said.

He stretched out his hand, and Sarina took it.

"Pleased to meet you too." He said, smiling warmly.

The others introduced themselves. Elan, Adian. They showed the warm acceptance Ervin had showed. Sarina felt like she had been pulled into the larger canopy of their huge relationship.

"Ah", she thought, "so this is what it feels like."

Dinner was tomato soup and oven-baked bread. Courtesy of Ervin. They sat out on the porch eating and chatting around the table.

"Ugh", Rosie groaned, placing her hand on her face.

"What?" Sarina asked. "The meal's great."

"Yeah, that great," Rosie replied, pointing at Ervin.

Ervin had a foolish grin on his face. Sarina's eyes fleeted from him to Rosie, and back to him again.

"Okay. I'm lost." Sarina said, finally conceding.

"What, I think, Rosie is trying to say", Ervin said, "is that yours truly is proudly behind today's marvellous dinner."

"There he goes again," Elan said.

Olivia laughed. Sarina sat graciously between stunned, and awe.

"You prepared this?" she asked.

Ervin's head dipped in a small bow.

"It's really wonderful. Such exquisite taste." Sarina gushed.

"You hear that?" Ervin asked, looking around the table. "But of course, Rosie won't. She's a perpetual hater."

Laughter sprouted from the table.

Sarina laughed, and then gradually, slipped into a smile. She looked around the table, and she felt roped into this warm gauze of affection wound around the people on the table. They smiled, laughed, chatted, with the same look in their eyes. And they gave her that look. The look of acceptance, of friendship, of family.

During the meal, they got to talk about Kyan.

"I don't get this," Adian said, a quizzical look on his face. "You mean to tell me, that he's lived most his life in solitude, and never knew of the existence of mermaids?"

"Yeah. That's what he told me." Sarina said. "And his reactions showed just that. I mean, he was shell shocked when he saw us."

"If he hasn't, then there's no way he's a harp guard. We should also consider that that could be affected. He could just be a poseur." Elan said.

Adrian *hmm*-ed his assent.

Ervin sat succumbed to pressing thoughts.

Soon, they had wrapped up dinner. And proceeded towards the beach for some quality jesting time.

They sat around a mild fire. And talked. The issue of Kyan somehow sprang up during their discussion, and they had to reach a consensus. To embark on a little swimming expedition. In search of Kyan.

Ervin, Elan, Rosie, and Olivia, went out to sea, leaving Adian behind with Vanessa and Sarina.

Adian busied himself with poking into the fire, stoking it, and causing it to burst into liveliness.

Sarina and Vanessa were on the other side engaged in quiet lively chat.

"So tell me", Sarina said, her eyes kindling with interest, "how does it feel dating a merman?"

Vanessa's eyes moved in their sockets. As though she were searching the air for answers.

"Uhm", she started, "I don't know if it's quite different for me. Because you know, I'm human and all that."

"Come on", Sarina cooed, "that doesn't mean anything. You and me, we're the same. The only difference is that one of us has a bit of the otherworldly tagged to our person. Take that out, and we're…" she rose her lower arms up, to the length of her shoulder blades, and shrugged, in a justifying way.

"Yeah," Vanessa said. And sighed.

"But really", Sarina said, "Tell me. I want to know."

Vanessa looked at her.

'Well, whatever I'm going to say is going to be from my perspective. I mean, dating a merman could mean different things for different people." She paused. Allowed the crackling of the fire to grow prominent for a bit, before speaking again.

"You see, being in love with a merman, is…" her eyes roved around the air, her lips slightly parted. Then she glanced across at Adian, bathed partly in the warm red of the fire, and partly in shadow. "You know sometimes you feel or you experience something, and you're like: this is the best thing that has ever happened to me?"

Sarina nodded.

"Well, this," she looked at Adian again, "this is more than that. It's like the universe is breathing especially on you while caressing you with divinity. It's nothing short of beautiful."

Sarina was completely immersed in Vanessa words as she continued, lost like one at sea, when Olivia and the rest walked into the light.

16

Sarina could see the water dripping down their bodies through the dull red glow of the fire. Their shadows, stretched at an angle, across the beach sand, danced with the flickering fire.

"So", Adian said, moving closer to them, "how'd it go?"

"We didn't see anything," Elan said. "We scoured through familiar waters. Even extended the scope, went a little out to sea. Nothing."

Sarina *hmm*-ed.

A part of her had been expectant, viewing the prospect of Kyan arrival with a tinge of trepidation. While the other part didn't want him to be found.

Well, now, she could not explain the feeling of disappointment that sank through her, pervading her entire being.

Adian heaved a sigh.

"Well let's just go inside. And call this a night. I'm certain we'll be seeing him."

"You are?" Sarina blurted.

Everyone looked at her.

"I mean", Adian said, "you girls saw him at sea, within familiar waters. I just get the feeling we may be seeing him soon. Maybe taking a swim, or coming to the beach for a curious walk.

"Oh. Okay." Sarina said.

"Ah. Let's call it a night then." Ervin said.

Inside the cottage, Rosie and Olivia were chatting and doing little work in the kitchen. Adian and Vanessa had left for their home, driving out in Vanessa's convertible. Elan had gone straight from the beach to his and Rosie's bungalow. Sarina had gone to bed upstairs.

Ervin walked towards them in the kitchen.

"Hey, girls." He greeted.

"Ervin", Rosie chirped.

"Mind if I join you?" he asked.

"Feel free. Anytime." Olivia said.

Ervin acknowledged her with an affectionate smile. Then he looked up the stairs.

"Sarina's..?" he cocked his brows questioningly.

"In her room. Asleep." Olivia said.

"Okay," Ervin said, then he moved closer to them.

"Is there a problem?" Rosie asked.

"I wouldn't call it a problem, you know. I just didn't want to say this around Sarina."

As if on cue, they both stopped washing the dishes, and turned towards him, giving him the full focus of their attention.

"You know, out there on the beach, even during dinner, I'd been thinking. Kyan. The name, the description, it rang a bell in my head. It wasn't till we were out to sea, that it became clear. I know him."

"What?" Rosie asked.

Olivia asked hers, by cocking her brows.

"Kyan", Ervin said, his voice lower than before, "I know him. From my childhood." He looked at the sisters, taking their thirsty eyes in.

"He was fast." Ervin continued. "Had the power of speed. We used to race then. And as expected, I'd always lose. But then one day he just disappeared."

"It's just as she said then," Olivia said, her face ripening with comprehension.

Rosie whispered,

"That means…", she fell into silence. A silence laden with

implicative meaning. They all knew the remaining words that refused to follow Rosie's whisper.

Rosie bid them good night, then walked out the cottage through the back. Ervin and Olivia walked towards the door that lead to their room. Olivia thrust a thought into Ervin's mind.

"How is it, that we all cross paths with those who have similar powers?" she asked.

"I don't know." Ervin thought back, then smiling he said *"Might be the powers of the universe at work. The very workings of fate."*

He curled an arm around Olivia's waist, as they disappeared through the door.

17

Two weeks later, Sarina sat alone at a table. She was in a sea-view restaurant. Those had begun springing up, like lilies, in specific spots in the village. Courtesy of the deluge of tourists and visitors from outside the village. And they were really good.

From time to time, the swash of the sea would call to her and she would fling her eyes into its fluid undulation. With her eyes, she would trace the curves and cusps, of every ripple-*y* mound jutting out the water, and melding into another one.

Someone laughed. A sound that felt very familiar, and as always, intrigued her. She turned and looked towards the bar, where the laugh had come from.

He was there, sitting, talking and laughing with another girl. The glasses of orange juice, he had gone to pick up from the bar, sat at the counter in front of him. Sarina took in the girl that sat beside him. Sand pepper hair, a sprinkle of freckles on her face, and long lashes. As he talked, she noticed the girl's lips widen in a fascinated smile.

"Yeah, he has that effect." Sarina thought.

"Oh, Elwick." She groaned in her mind.

The first time she had seen him, he was one of two strangers who had walked into Rosie's shop to check out her products. That was the morning Rosie and Olivia had left her in the shop, to go make wedding arrangements. That was the morning she had been elated at the thought that one of them could be her protector. And she was right. The one who had given her a cheeky smile before leaving, she saw more of. The other one vanished, like night in the advent of daylight.

He had walked up to her, one mild evening at the pub.

"Hi." He had greeted, settling into the chair opposite her.

One look at the person who had just greeted her was all it took for Sarina's heart to launch into a tirade of beats. His hazel brown eyes with long dark lashes He had that cheeky smile on. Sarina felt like she was dust, and she was being blown away in a gradual stream.

However, she managed a 'hi' in response.

"I'm Elwick." He said, bending his hand to gesture to himself. "And you are?"

"Sarina." She had responded.

At first, he had been the one holding the wheels in a conversation that sounded more like an interview. He asked questions that was juicy with eagerness, and Sarina would supply answers rather timidly. He would lean into the table, staring at Sarina like he could not get enough of her. At those moments, Sarina would feel tremors pass through her heart, and a mask of heat grow on her face.

Elwick had spoken softly, almost tentatively, like he was leading a child on their first walk.

And then as the clock tick-tocked, Sarina began to peek out her timidity, like a blossoming flower in spring. It started with giggles, then laughter, and comments of her own. Till they were in a ripe conversation, filled with laughter, jokes, and other light banter.

He had walked her to the cottage that night, and she had slept with her heart fleeting through clouds.

They had seen each other. Like almost every day. Sarina' heart would prance within her chest when she was not with Elwick. And would settle into chanting sweet notes, when she was around him. All the while, she could feel him doting on her, treating her like a screen of water cupped graciously in his palms.

Until, one day, he had taken her out to a restaurant by the seaside, and asked her out.

The sun had peeked through the edge of the roof, bathing the restaurant, or at least, the place they sat, in golden light. The sea was singing, gulls calling, the sea-breeze smoothing its way across her skin. And then he asked her out. Her heart racing, fleet-footed and nimbly through massive expanses of pure excitement, Sarina had said yes. And then had spent coming weeks enthused by Elwick, and being charmed. But now.

She looked at him again. No longer feeling as ecstatic about their relationship as she had been. It had taken her almost two weeks, for the padding of attachment to Elwick to begin wearing off. She began picking out things in Elwick. Things she had not seen before. It was like water was splashing on her, sluicing a cocoon of dirt from off her.

Elwick was a sucker for the nick of his appearance. He would stop by every sheet of glass, regardless of its size, flatten his hair out, and palm it into a specific curve, brush a finger across his brows, and lick his lips, in exactly that order. He always made sure his shirts stopped a few buttons below the curve of his muscular chest. And when he got into any room, he was bound to leave the girls fawning at his wake. Sarina did not have a problem with the way he threw smiles to every girl or passed comments that skirted the fringes of flirtation. But as time went on, she began to see these things. They poked once at her eyes. How could she not notice them?

She came back to the present. Elwick was standing up now. He ran his fingers across his slick black hair and licked his lips in a manner Sarina thought was inviting. The sand-pepper haired girl's eyes followed Elwick as he stood. She smiled, and placed a hand on his wrist, then she said something to which Elwick laughed. He grabbed the glasses of orange juice and ice from the counter and turned towards where Sarina sat. She averted her gaze immediately. And then pretended to be engrossed in the dancing sea.

She heard the thud of his boots on the wooden restaurant floor. They got louder as he approached until they stopped.

"Hey, gorgeous. Orange juice with ice." He said, placing the glasses on the table.

"Hey", Sarina said, extricating her eyes from the sea, and flicking them up to him.

She smiled.

Elwick dragged out a chair and sat. Then he sipped at his juice.

He closed his eyes and hmm-ed.

"It's good, right?" he asked opening his eyes.

"Yeah, yeah," Sarina said, sipping hers for the first time. "Very good. A sweet relief from the rigours of the day."

Elwick stretched his hand across the table and placed them on Sarina's.

"Come on", he said, his voice moistening with concern, "tell me about your day. I want to hear everything."

Sarina felt a gentle flush in her heart. A mockery of the

excitement she had felt some weeks back at Elwick's touch.

She found his gaze surprisingly disturbing. Probably because she wanted to tell him that she did not like this restaurant. That she wanted to be someplace else. Maybe at the beach. Somewhere where they could just be alone, together, without him having to flirt with every girl in sight. She wanted to tell him that he was so obsessed with himself most of the time, that she could not say some things to him. Except for cases like now, when he asked.

Sarina wanted to say all these. But when she opened her mouth, an almost diary-like account of her day was what crawled out instead.

She had thought, "Maybe all this is, this flirtation, the self-obsession, could just be his friendly, outgoing qualities."

Elwick listened with rapt attention. He could never know the pain that underlined Sarina's speech. The one she fought to keep buried.

Perhaps if Olivia were anywhere close, she could give him a lengthy sermon, on let-down emotions.

18

"Holla, girls. This lunch's not going to eat itself." Rosie said at the top of her voice.

Her voice carried through the spaciousness of the living room. Sarina shouted something inaudible from upstairs. Olivia did the same downstairs. Rosie groaned and walked out. She walked towards the beach, to where a mat lay, neatly spread over a section of the sandy ground.

She looked at the mat, looked at her surroundings, and *hmm*-ed satisfactorily.

The sun was warm, and soft today, deciding to keep the sharpness of its rays to itself. The sky was an azure canvass replete with pillows of white.

Rosie cast one look towards the cottage and saw approaching figures.

"Finally", she said out loud.

She began unloading plates from the huge basket she had brought with her.

"This is going to be some lunch," Olivia said, immediately she arrived at the spot.

She ran her fingers affectionately through Rosie's hair and sat on the mat. Sarina followed suit.

"Who's to say we can't have a little outdoor lunching while the boys are off to something else," Rosie said.

Olivia and Sarina cheered. Then they burst into laughter.

After lunch, Sarina decided to explore the beach a little. On her own, this time. Her eyes roamed around the beach, taking in as much of its length as it could, until it fell on a formation of rocks, just off the cliffs, at a corner of the beach. She walked towards the formation of rocks.

As she got closer, the formation of rocks began to appear more visible. And then she realized. It was not just a formation of rocks. It was more than that. Sarina walked, moving closer and closer. Stopping, only when she had gotten to within a few feet from the rock formation.

"I was not wrong after all." She thought.

Sarina inhaled and exhaled deeply. Standing, along the fringes of the water, with a colony of rocks clinging to its sides, was the entrance to a cave. Water from the sea flowed in and flowed out as the waves crashed and ebbed. Sarina looked around, then stepped into the water.

The water rippled as her feet waded through. She stopped when she was at the mouth of the cave. She could hear the regular plop of water falling in drops. It was made resonant by the hollowness of the cave. Sarina moved further in.

The inside of the cave was not as dark as Sarina had thought. As her irises adjusted, the walls of the cave took on a little glow. The walls was lumpy and rocky, made smooth by water cascading down it. Sarina got closer to them, and noticed that the glow in the cave was caused by the water on the walls. The water, as it slithered down the wall, shimmered, giving the cave an otherworldly effect. Sarina looked at the walls with awe. She was taken in by this display of natural beauty.

Sarina moved closer to the walls, and tentatively, brushed her fingers against it. Her fingers slid gracefully across the wet hardness of the wall. Her eyes rolled down to where the line of water lapped at the wall. Then she squinted. She thought she had seen something. She stooped and took her face closer to the wall. Her eyes widened. She had indeed seen something.

There were writings on the wall, resting close to the water level. The words were glossy. She passed her fingers across them. They were smooth, one with the wall.

"Not engraved." Sarina thought.

The words had to have been written on the wall with some kind of ink. She looked closer, inspecting them. Her eyes ran from one word to the other, connecting them, in her head.

Your name is written in the stars.

Sarina's mind began to spin, like a loom.

"Who wrote this?" she asked herself. "And for whom."

Her mind ticked and tocked, making conjectures and flinging them away if found unreasonable.

"Could it be Ervin?" she thought. "Did he write it for Olivia?"

"Maybe it was Elan." She thought after a while. "He probably did this for Rosie."

She, however, could not outpace the feeling of uncertainty that yapped at her heels. Without concrete answers to her questions, she allowed herself to be subdued by uncertainty.

The cave was a little one. So she moved further in, her eyes searching the walls for some more scribbling. She found one more.

I have more love for you than there is sand on the beach.

She reached its end and turned back.

Sarina took one more look at the writing on the wall, before she walked out of the cave, and into the brightness of day.

The sound of voices hit her, soft and light, as if coming from afar. She flung her eyes forward and saw Ervin and Olivia in the water chatting with someone.

Sarina's heart leapt.

It had just dawned on her the identity of the person Ervin and Olivia were chatting with. Blonde hair. Strong swimmers build. Ocean eyes. They were all too familiar.

"What's he doing here?" she thought, her eyes unable to leave Kyan.

19

Kyan had ballooned out the surface of the undulating sea. He squinted, letting his eyes get accustomed to the glare of the sun. He bobbed in the water, the end of his tail making little squiggly movements. His mind had been replete with thoughts and images of Sarina since he had seen her a few days ago. Try as he might, he could not get her out of his head.

He looked to shore, puffed out water that had slithered down his face into his mouth. Then, sinking smoothly below the surface, he succumbed to his impulses. He moved towards shore. He needed to see her.

The only thing signalling Kyan's presence in the sea, was the gentle ripple, like the trail of a comet, snaking across the surface, as he swam gently. No sooner had he brought his head out the water than he stopped abruptly. His eyes stared straight ahead, fixed. Fixed on someone. An incredulous look decorated his face. Playing, not too far from him, was a couple. A merman and a mermaid. He did not carry incredulity for the mermaid as much as he did for the merman.

Kyan's lips trembled slightly. Like the barbs of a feather, twitching under a light breeze.

"Ervin." He called, his voice spiced with uncertainty.

Kyan had not expected his voice to travel that far. But it did. Because just then, the merman turned, a huge grin on his face.

Kyan blinked. The look on his face switched fluidly from incredulity to surprise. He watched the grin ebb out of Ervin's face. A burst of shock and recognition swooped in, reanimating his face.

Then Ervin's mouth opened, and a short spiky laugh, heavy with unbelief, fell out.

"Ervin," Kyan called, this time somewhat stronger.

He noticed, vaguely, the mermaid beside Ervin flashing them both a confused look.

Ervin swam forward. Kyan swarm forward. And they swam into an embrace, like opposite sides of two magnets. No one painted a more perfect scene of the reconciliation of long lost friends than the both of them.

"Ervin!" Kyan exclaimed, his voice heightened with excitement. "How?" he asked.

"Leave the 'how' for later, and tell me how you're here?" Ervin said, laughing.

Kyan laughed.

"Something dragged me up shore. Something quite alluring." He said.

"What's that? You after a quarry?" Ervin asked.

"No. Definitely not a quarry."

Ervin made to speak, when he was interrupted.

"Is there a problem, hun?" Olivia asked, placing a hand on Ervin's shoulder, and stopping just beside him.

She had noticed that the man with whom Ervin was all smiles, was the one they had ran from some few days ago. The one he had said had been a friend of his from childhood.

Kyan looked at the mermaid that stayed beside Ervin. Besides her apparent splendour, he also noticed that she was one of the mermaids he had seen with Sarina.

"Hello", he greeted with a smile.

"Urgh", Ervin groaned and dropped his palm across his face. "How silly of me."

"Silly, indeed," Kyan said from the corner of his mouth, his eyes still fixated on Olivia. His lips pursed into a tight smile. "I believe introductions are in order."

"Uhm," Ervin began, "Olivia, this is Kyan, my friend from childhood. I believe you two have met, under unpleasant circumstances. Well, just to clear the air, Kyan is a good guy." He turned to Kyan, and making a referring gesture towards Olivia with his hand, said,

"And this, this dame beside me, is Olivia. My fiancée."

Kyan's eyes brightened with surprise. His eyes ran from Ervin to Olivia, and from Olivia back to Ervin.

"A big congratulations to you both." He said.

"Thank you", Olivia said.

"It's nice meeting you, for the second time, Olivia." He said, stretching out his arm for a handshake.

Olivia smiled.

"The pleasure is mine." She replied, taking his hand.

Ervin and Kyan burst into excited chatter, trying to catch up with lost times. Along the line of their conversation, Olivia tugged gently at Ervin's hair, bending his head so his ear would get closer to her mouth. Then she whispered something to him. His eyes perked up, and he gave a sharp nod.

"Yeah, Kyan, Olivia and I, are inviting you to our wedding."

Kyan smiled.

"Wow. This honour is huge."

Olivia and Ervin smiled.

"Hey, Vanessa", Olivia called out.

Kyan looked to the direction Olivia's eyes were fixed. He saw a lady, with long curly black hair and blue eyes, swimming in the water. By her swimming strokes, he discerned that she was not a mermaid.

"You boys are going to have to excuse me." She said.

She patted Ervin on the arm before leaving, and said a sharp goodbye to Kyan, before swimming off to join Vanessa.

Kyan watched her swim towards the human girl. By the way, the two of them mingled: the glee on the girl's face and the level of normalcy on her face, as she swam with a girl who was half fish, half-human, he could tell that they were friends. Tight friends.

He turned back to Ervin, who was still speaking.

"My old friend," Ervin said, placing a hand on Kyan's shoulder. "I really have somewhere that I must be in this moment."

They stared each other long in the face, the memory of past times floating at the surface of their eyes.

"You know, I'll perfectly understand if you do not attend my wedding. With the whole landwalker thing that will age you, and all." Ervin sighed. "I guess what I'm saying is I'd understand if you don't want to take that chance."

There was a short stint of silence between them both.

"Do you think it's worth it? Becoming a landwalker?" Kyan asked, breaking the silence. His voice was low and gentle, like he was teetering on an edge, on the brink of surrendering to something.

Ervin looked away from them to where Olivia swam. His eyes took her in, in a particularly holistic way. And like always, he got that rush, a minty flush of satisfaction, of bliss, of peace. Of love.

"When you find love, absolutely." His voice was dreamy and ecstatic.

"Beside as long as you keep returning back to the sea, land shouldn't age you'' he added.

It was as if he had torn himself out from the uterus of another phase when he looked away from Olivia, because when he spoke next, his voice was cheery.

"You know, I took the risk a few number of times. Came out to land, looked for love. But there was none, no woman, that arrested my heart like Olivia."

Ervin looked back to where Olivia was wading through the water.

Just then, Kyan notices a movement by the corner of his eye. Kind of like the quirk of a spec. He flicked his eyes towards the direction of the movement. And they did not come back. In truth, they were held. Spellbound.

He had just spotted Sarina coming out of a cave.

Kyan felt his heart beat faster, like the rattle of a rattlesnake rising to a crescendo.

Ervin did not notice the distraction of his audience. His own eyes were fixed on Olivia.

"Is she a new mermaid?"

"What?" Ervin asked, flicking his eyes back to Kyan.

He noticed Kyan's eyes looking somewhere else. He turned, looking towards the direction of Kyan's gaze. And he saw Sarina.

"Oh, her? Yeah, she is. She's a cousin to Olivia and Rosie."

Ervin crinkled his face up in confusion.

"I thought you'd met already?" he asked.

"Yeah. Not met, like met. For instance, I met Olivia today, like got to really know her. When I met her, her name was the only thing I could get from her. She was terrified for some reason."

"Ah. You can't blame any of us. We've unfortunately had numerous encounters with Quintess's guards in the past. In retrospect, we can't be more guarded, and alert." Ervin said, with a shrug.

"You know what?" Ervin said with a surge, his eyes lighting up with the spark of an idea. "You could help us, you know?"

"Yeah. Doing what?" Kyan asked.

"Since you stay in the sea, you could keep an eye out there for us. You know alert us, if any of the harp guards decide to use the sea, as an alternative route."

"You mean they haven't come through here before?" Kyan asked, his eyes wide open.

"Nah. Not really. Most of the time, they came through land. They seemed to have used the sea only once. And that was in our last encounter."

"Hope no one got hurt?" Kyan asked.

Ervin *hmm*-ed.

"We could have. Mostly the brunt of getting hurt, or worse, killed, lies with the girls. They're the one Quintess is after. Well, the harp guards kidnapped, Vanessa, our human friend. Used her as leverage to get to us. But they were going to kill her anyway. They proved that when they dunked her into the sea and attacked."

Kyan flung his eyes towards where Vanessa was, her limbs splashing into the water, as she made swimming strokes.

"Obviously", Kyan said, "you people got your heads out of it."

"Yeah, thanks to Adian. We were completely overwhelmed. Vanessa would have died if he had not stepped in. I had sent a telepathic message to the sea animals to bring her up, but it was difficult holding the link in place while staving off attacks."

"He's that strong, huh?' Kyan asked.

"Yeah. He shocked us. I mean, shocked us enough, to make Elan have a change of heart." Ervin's eyes went up manner-of-factly.

"Change of heart?" Kyan asked.

"That's a story for another time, Kyan. I mean, this way you get to swim towards shore. Even if it's to hear stories."

Kyan laughed and tapped Ervin on his shoulder.

Kyan flashed a look towards where he had seen Sarina. There was nothing. Just the open maw of the cave, halved by the inflow of water at the bottom.

Kyan felt his spirits sink a few inches away from rock bottom. He tried, however, to gauge those feeling from reflecting on his face.

He bade Ervin an affected farewell, then turned, and began to move silkily through the water. Ervin wore a gentle smile on his face, as he watched Kyan sink under the water. He saw a ripple on the surface of the water, snaking out. Farther and farther into sea. Until it disappeared from the coffer of his sight.

20

E rvin had just set foot on the beach from the water when he heard someone's voice.

"Hey."

He looked up and saw Adian walking towards him.

"Hey." Ervin greeted. "What's up?"

They shook hands. Then Adian ran his eyes around their environment, surveying for unwanted ears. Satisfied that there was no one near them. He brought the focus of his attention back on Ervin.

"Yeah", he began, "so I just came in from the village."

"Yeah?" Ervin said, his voice laden with expectancy.

"You know, the men Sarina had told Rosie and Olivia she saw that day in Rosie's shop?"

"Yeah", Ervin replied, "the one's she couldn't get her mind off."

"Exactly. Those ones. Well, we know already that one of them, Elwick, came to protect her. The other one, now, is a harp guard."

"Are you serious?" Ervin asked, a disturbed look on his face.

"I wouldn't be telling you this if I wasn't," Adian said.

Ervin ran his fingers over his hair. His eyes fidgeted in their sockets. He opened his mouth to speak, shut them, and walked a few paces away from Adian. He turned and walked back.

"So?" he asked.

Adian looked at him.

"He's spent such a long time here."

"Yeah? You would have thought he would have made an attempt on Sarina's life yet?" he said with exasperation, flinging his arms up and letting them fall back to his sides.

"That's the thing," Adian said. "I think after our last encounter, they're a bit wary about attacking head-on. He's been here for weeks."

"And we're only just discovering this now," Ervin said.

"Exactly," Adian said, nodding.

A wave of silence washed over them. Ervin's eyes took on the distracted look of one whose mind was spinning furiously. Finally, like one breaking out a reverie, he flicked his eyes towards Adian. Adian stared back into his eyes.

"There's bound to be more," Adian said.

Ervin walked a few paces away. Stopped, raked his fingers through his hair. Then he made an akimbo and turned back to where Adian was standing.

"Now, what're we going to do?" he asked.

21

Elwick descended the slope rolling on to the beach. He had been watching Sarina from atop the hills. A harp guard had tried to follow after her but Elwick had successfully attacked him. He had seen her go in a cave, and come out. And had then seen her walk away. He had gone to the cottage where he had almost knocked his knuckles out, and still yet had gotten no response. It was not until he reached for the knob and twisted that he noticed that the door was locked. Turning, he could see figures out on the beach, about two of them. Placing his palm over his eyes, to cut out the rays of the sun, he made out the familiar figure of Elan.

"Hey, Elan." He called on getting to the beach.

Elan had his arms around Rosie's waist, and they were pointing at something at sea. He turned to the voice calling his name, and smiled when he saw Elwick.

"Elwick", he called, withdrawing his arm from around Rosie's waist. "What brings you here?"

"Nothing special. Just hi-s and hellos."

They shake hands.

"Hello, Rosie." Elwick greeted.

"Elwick." Rosie reciprocated by dipping her head to the side.

"A beautiful afternoon at the beach, huh?" Elwick said.

"You can say that," Rosie replied.

Elan and Elwick fell into light chatter, where they got to talk about home and their families. They were not tight in the way of friends, but they had met one of those times when Elan had been taken by his father to sea. Elwick's father was also one of the Light Queen's generals. By virtue of their fathers, connected by the time the men spent pondering over maps, and stratagems, their children had to form a bond, even if it was one as fragile as sun-beaten bones.

As they talked, Elwick caught, from the corner of his eye, Sarina walking past. He paused a bit and waved to her. She waved back, and he smiled. A cheeky grin. The same one he flashed at her. And all other girls. Sarina's lips curved in a tight smile, then she turned and moved away.

Elwick turned back to his conversation, after having made a mental note to check up on Sarina later.

22

I t seemed like a nice day to swim close to shore. That's what Kyan thought. And that's why he was telling himself he was going close to shore. But deep down the thick foliage of pretense, the truth pulsated like a beating heart. Sarina. She was like a lighthouse, standing tall, and exuding a magnetic attraction. And like metal fillings, he found his mind running back to her. No matter the direction he had stirred it to.

He bobbed in the water, and then stretched his sights towards shore. He could see it, a sandy slip at a distance. He moved forward, flicking his arms while making gentle flaps with his tail.

Sarina would never understand Elwick's thing for sea view bars. She had harangued herself, citing his being a merman as the reason. But then, any of Ervin, Elan, or Adian, would stand as proof that her feelings were not unfounded. She wanted to be someplace, less open. A café, the pub, a cosy Italian restaurant somewhere inland. Yet, here she was.

Gulls wailed and called to themselves. It was like an orchestra of trumpet-*y* conversations. Breeze blew, beating her maroon dress, and forcing it against her body. A strand of her long blue hair danced into her vision. She reached out with her fingers and tucked it in with the rest of its family.

Elwick was sitting across from her, saying some nice things to the waitress. Sarina pretended that the rich smile Elwick lavished on the waitress did not cause something of a stab to her heart. Or the blush on the waitress's cheeks did not make little seedlings of anger sprout from inside her. What started as an order for two lemonades, derailed into an exchange of pleasantries and compliments.

Sarina entwined her fingers. Disentangled them. And twined them back again. She continued the sequence, trying to merge happily into the background. She looked towards the sea and sighed. Why was she lacking the sense of fulfilment and happiness, she thought would fill her, as she went down this trail with Elwick?

There was a freckle of people at the village beach. Kyan slowed to a stop, taking in the beach again. He sighed. There was no way he was going on to shore with this many people around. He decided to just hover close to the beach where he could see what was happening, and at the same time, draw no attention. Anyone seeing him from the beach would be seeing a regular swimmer, chest-deep in water.

He felt that pull in his heart again. That sense of growth, a protuberance inside him, dragging him towards something. His eyes caressed the beachside until they settled on a bar. The bar was high up the bank, with an extended enclosure wherein sat tables sat. Some of the tables, he noticed, had people on them. Pretty waitresses sauntered in between the bar and the tables, taking orders, and satisfying them.

He had almost taken his eyes off the bar, when he caught the familiar shine of blue hair. He squinted, and then his eyes eased.

"Sarina", he thought. "She's with him."

He looked at Elwick, talking to a waitress, while Sarina withered into oblivion, and he felt a stab of sadness.

"Just what does she see in him?" he wailed in his heart.

Every time he had seen them out on a date, nine out of ten, Elwick was flirting with some other girl. And every time, there would be a surge of emotions. One of which would be how extremely inadequate Elwick was for Sarina. In Kyan's eyes, Sarina was deserving, deserving of so much more.

Staring at the both of them, Kyan assuaged his hurt with the conviction that he and Sarina were destined for each other. Whatever it is she and Elwick seemed to have, was nothing. A trifle. A smokescreen.

Kyan retreated further into the water, then sank below its surface.

132

Sarina's eyes flicked towards the water. She felt a strange tug in her heart. She had seen something from the corner of her eye. Now that she looked, there was nothing. Just the sea billowing with waves. She flicked her hair, and looked back at Elwick. He was still talking to the waitress.

"Darling", she called, somewhat exasperatedly.

23

Kyan ran his hand over the wet smoothness of the cave walls. The cave had assumed some sort of significance for him, since he had seen Sarina walk out from there some time ago. He went deeper into the cave, his fingers brushing against the walls. His eyes roamed the arched roof of the cave, the beautiful display of shiny water dripping off its surface, the hollow plops as the water dropped; all of which had become familiar to him. All of which constituted a salve of comfort. He felt most happy here. At peace. The sea did not feel like home anymore. Land did not offer much in the way of hospitability either. It was like every time he tried to go on there, Elwick was there. Like a ghost, he haunted him, making him feel angry and resentful, every time. But here, in this cave, he felt an overwhelming sense of normalcy click into place. Perhaps, the sense of normalcy he felt, owed to the residues of Sarina's presence stuck in the cave, like paint coating.

So he took to coming here anytime he came close to shore. The cave aroused in him that feeling of a connection between him and Sarina. He ran his hands over an array of gleaming words on the walls of the cave. Kyan's eyes ran over the words, calling out each one in with the backing of solid emotions.

24

Days flew by. The cottage was seeing a burst of activity, as everyone prepped up for Olivia's wedding. The boys were away doing their own thing. Same for the girls. And time rolled on and on, until the eve of Olivia's wedding came knocking. And with it, Olivia's hen party.

A portion of the beach was bathed in the soft red of a sizeable bonfire. The waves shambled towards shore, lapping at the edge of the beach, while light from the fire reflected off its surface in broken pieces. There was a little shack, hastily built by the boys earlier in the day. There were a handful of girls in it, with the rest spilling out to the open beach. There was mild music, inflected with a bout of comfortable chatter.

"Okay, okay, everyone," Rosie called. "Hey", she called, pointing at the girl in charge of the music and signalling for her to wind it down.

"Thank you", she said, when the music had gone down several

notches. "Now gather again, girls. This is a spicy treat. My spicy treat." She turned her head from side to side, making sure she had everyone's attention.

"Tarot and oracle cards." She cried in a sharp quick burst, popping out a hand full of cards simultaneously.

Cheers, giggles, and a scattering of applause broke out amongst the little crowd. Then the girls huddled around Rosie, in a large circle, as she spread the cards, very expertly.

"These are my special mermaid oracle cards. Who's up?" she asked.

The girls surged closer, clamouring softly for a chance.

The girls took turns getting their fortunes read, and gradually the pool of unread dwindled.

"Hey, that reminds me," Rosie said suddenly. "Guess what?" she asked, giving everyone a quizzical look.

"You just saw your fortune?" Olivia blurted.

There was a drizzle of laughter.

"Nice try, Oly," Rosie said. "Come on, people. Nobody?"

"Come on, Rosie. You know we don't have all night." Vanessa said, looking at her imploringly.

Rosie cast hopeful glances around for a few moments. Everyone had the same look. Solicitous. Expectant. Answerless.

"Okay." She said, after seeing that no one was forthcoming.

"Guess who's next in line to get married." She said, her voice taking a slight twist of taunting. She lifted her right hand into the air and twirled her fingers.

Miriam was the first one to notice the light from the fire catch on something on Rosie's finger. She squinted.

"What's that?" she asked herself.

Her eyes perked up with recognition, just as an excited scream rent the mini-silence.

"Oh my God," Olivia exclaimed, rushing to Rosie's side, and taking her hand. "Have you been hiding this?."

She manoeuvred Rosie's fingers in hers until she held the finger. Vanessa, Sarina, Cara, Miriam, and the rest of the girls had rushed in by now. Olivia's fingers closed in on the diamond-lined with aquamarine stones on a simple silver band coiled around Rosie's finger. It glistened with pristine beauty.

"How?" she asked, casting Rosie a cheery, and inquisitive look.

"Yeah, tell us how," Vanessa said, hugging her from behind. "Who wants to hear Rosie tell a story?"

Everyone cheered. Rosie laughed.

"Okay, okay." She said.

The laughter faded out as Rosie opened her mouth to speak.

"Okay. So, I and Elan are walking along the top of the cliffs, talking, playing, you know, the usual. When he says, 'hey isn't it beautiful?'. And I'm like: 'What?'. And he says, 'The sunset.' So I look over towards the ocean. And not that I haven't noticed before, but you know, it's the sunset. Its beauty shocks you every time."

Her audience nodded. Grunts of affirmation even went up in some places. Rosie continued.

"I tell him it's beautiful. But then I turn, and my heart like punches against my chest. There's Elan. On one knee." Her voice had climbed up a few notches now, her eyes tearing up, as she relived the moment in her memory.

Her face had heated up, her mouth open, with her lips slightly twisted, as waves of astonishment tore through her entire being. Elan's eyes were pools of resolution, promise, and love.

"Rosie," he said, reaching out with his free arm, and clutching her hand in his. "My life has been nothing short of extraordinary since you came into it. If the stars can hear me, I twinkle back at them every day, with gratitude, for knotting us both together. And I would love for this extraordinariness, which is you, to go on for the rest of my life."

Elan paused, staring deep into Rosie's eyes, letting the effect of what he had just said seep in.

Rosie's mind was spinning, taking in huge gulps the truth of what was actually happening. She felt like she would choke soon.

"Rosie", Elan called, "will you marry me?"

Rosie did not remember screaming yes. She only remembered

losing herself in a long emotional kiss, heavy with meaning, and the feeling that they would be together. For as long as they lived.

Even now, narrating it to the girls, she could still feel the rush in her head. It was like a slight buzz.

The girls poured in their congratulations. Olivia, Vanessa, and Sarina wrapped her up in a group embrace.

Rosie resumed reading her cards soon after the kerfuffle had died down. Soon Sarina was up.

Sarina knelt closer to Rosie, resting, with her butt across the flat of her legs.

"Okay, your turn, Sarina", Rosie said, arranging the cards on the table.

Rosie spread the cards down and asked Sarina to place her hands on them and close her eyes. Rosie then gathered the cards and did some sorting, and then came up with a sequence of cards. She flicked her eyes toward Sarina.

"What?" Sarina asked.

Rosie looked back at the cards, and back to Sarina.

"Okay," Rosie began, "this is it. Overall, Elwick's not good news."

"What?" Sarina asked, her demeanour dropping several degrees.

"I mean, Elwick is not the right one in your, you know, romantic relationship. He won't bring you that bliss, happiness, and love you so desire."

Rosie sighed.

"See, Sarina", she said. "I, myself, don't feel good about him. I mean, I have reservations about you two. Even without the cards saying it."

Sarina's eyes jittered.

"Is that all?" she asked. Her voice was low.

"No, no," Rosie said, flicking her attention back to the cards.

"It's not all sad, Sarina." Rosie picked a card up.

"That happiness and romance you seek is ahead of you. It says here that there's going to be a reconciliation, very soon, with your true love."

"Oh", Sarina said, not sure if she should feel better or lapse into worse as her past lovers had been nothing but a sea of disappointment.

Olivia, who had been close to them the whole time, wrapped her arms sympathetically around Sarina's shoulders. She felt bad that Sarina had gotten out of a sour relationship to jump into one that was just as sour. She kissed Sarina on the top of her head, and closed her eyes. Olivia did not want to worsen Sarina's condition. She had heard things. Things about Elwick. They were flying around village circles. Mostly the female village circles. All the details of the hearsay pointed to him being an avid womanizer.

Olivia wished she could reach out to Sarina's heart and soothe out the pain. More than anything, she wished Sarina would break up with Elwick.

25

Kyan tucked his hands into his pockets as his legs regained their strength and he relaxed into his stride. His eyes went to the sky, an immense moonless sheet of dark sticky blue, with a freckle of stars. The beachside was almost empty. He could hear the song of the waves crashing against the cliffs. He had come on to show a few minutes ago. Ervin had left him some clothes at the cave. Just like he had said he would. He thought of Ervin and a smile came to his face.

"That's one person to rely on", he thought.

While walking, he heard the faint sounds of music, and laughter wafting across to him and pervading the silence of the beach. He took a turn, coming out a profile of rocks, and saw a glow of red in the distance. It was a fire, a fire at the beach. He squinted and picked out a shack and a group of girls hanging out. As he got closer, the sound from the merriment got louder.

Kyan made sure to shy away from the light, sticking to the

shadows to remain unseen. He noticed that it was an all-girls party. Then it dawned on him. The wedding was tomorrow.

"Must be Olivia's bachelorette party." He thought.

Just then, he looked towards the cottage and saw someone coming up towards it. The surrounding hillside was bathed in darkness, but he could still see. Very clearly. That was one of the quirks of being a merman. All those time in the depths of the sea, no moonlight, no sunshine, could sharpen the sight to heightened degrees of clarity.

Whoever it was, creeping towards the cottage, and looking around suspiciously, was not either of Adian, Elan, or Ervin. And Kyan could see that. He flicked a glance towards the partying girls, then hurried, clandestinely, towards the cottage.

The closer Kyan got, the louder his intuition screamed. The stranger was a guard of Quintess.

Kyan got closer and closer, and then he kicked a rock.

The man stilled. Then in the flick of a second, he turned and sprang towards Kyan. Like a tiger.

26

Yeah, come on guys." Ervin called. "Hey, Adian, take that corner."

The mermen, Ervin, Adian, and Elan were setting up the tent for the wedding, while the girls partied. Flashbulbs sat in the beach sand, spitting out beams of light, and providing illumination for their work.

"Ahaa", Ervin said, his voice tinged with satisfaction. "Yeah, that way, like that." He told Elan.

They were too engrossed in setting up the tent. They could not know that at that same moment, someone had tried to break into the cottage and that Kyan was trying to repel the person.

All the years spent, hunting at the bottom of the sea, and harnessing his power paid off. A normal person would have been tackled to the ground as soon as the harp guard had lurched. It was too sudden. However, at the nick of the second, Kyan spun out of the way. He moved like lightning zapping across the sky. Kyan spun towards the harp guard just as he was landing on the ground. Kyan dashed towards where the guard lay, already trying to spring to his feet. Placing a knee on the guard's left arm, Kyan grabbed the other arm and twisted it behind the guard.

The guard grunted with pain, relinquishing any ideas to struggle. He had been pinned. And very effectively at that.

Kyan closed his eyes holding out his bracelet and then whispered a spell, one his grandfather had taught him. The harp guard, in a blink, grew translucent, fading, till he winked out.

Kyan got to his feet. He was heaving furiously. He looked down to the beach. Everything was going on, undisturbed. Further down the beach, he saw the boys working at pulling up a tent. He then could make out the figure of Elwick, chatting up one of the girls from Olivia's party in his usual flirtatious manner.

He placed his hands on his hips, and with a puff, exhaled into the night air.

27

Sunset at the beach today, met some additional touch of magic and beauty. The horizon was a burst of soft orange, melding into the dusky blue of a larger portion of the sky. The sun was a ball of dull red sloth-*ing* towards the edge of the sea. The waves were soft and calm. It was as though they were giving their admiration to all the love going on on the beach.

It was Olivia and Ervin's wedding.

A big white tent sat on the beach, resting on ornate silver stilts that dug into the sandy ground. There were rings of flowers hanging on pegs at the entrance to the test. People milled around in the beach, wearing suits, and dresses, talking in couples, threesomes, and in much larger groups.

Inside the tent, there were about a dozen ornate candelabra's lining both walls. Ervin and Olivia had just concluded their vows and were consummating their wedding with a kiss. People oohed, and the clip-clap of applause broke out in the tent. Elan and Adian, stood to one side of the aisle, all on cream-coloured suits with bow ties, while Rosie and Vanessa, stood to the other side, with vinaceous dresses, and cream-coloured brooches. Olivia's grandparents sat at the front of the row of chairs, smiling, and clapping.

While Ervin and Olivia's lips were locked, Oliva lifted up her arms and threw out the bouquet in her hand.

The crowd gasped, cheered, and then clapped. Rosie and Vanessa turned towards Sarina. They gave her an excited smile, flicking their eyes to the bouquet in her hand. Sarina smiled, then looked down from mild embarrassment.

"Oh come here", Rosie said, opening her arms.

Rosie and Vanessa went in, swallowing Sarina in an embrace.

A live band began to play music.

By the time the wedding proper had wrapped up, the sun had sunk below the horizon. Only a streak of orange could be seen at the edge of a sky that was a field of stars. Ervin and Olivia marched out of the tent, with their train following right behind them. Then every other person dogging their tail. All ways led to the reception.

There were candles by the sides, abutting the path that led up to the cottage. Up there was sat another tent. This one was much larger, the fairy lights glowing from inside, made it look like a really bright flame in the dark. Music was wafting out from inside, inflecting the atmosphere of the hillside in melodious magic.

An additional stream of people poured in, swelling the numbers of guests from the wedding. Bursting out from the tent, was not only the sound of music but a delicious aroma, soft, yet strong, carrying along with it the promise of a rainbow of exquisite tastes inside.

"Oh my God. This is so good." One of the guests, a woman wearing a blue dress, said.

"Oh yeah. One can even say they're full already." Another guest said.

The woman laughed, then went inside the tent.

There was an array of round tables with chairs to each, neatly arranged in squads. The bride, the groom, and their friends and family, sat along a long table at the space in front reserved just for them. The music band played at their far left. The instruments – violin, cello, guitar, saxophone, drums, piano – merged fluidly into an ensemble of auditory beauty. At the right, lining the walls of the tent was a mini-bar. The cases were stacked with a laudable catalogue of drinks. Further towards the entrance, left of the doorway, was a huge buffet, consisting of food and confectionaries. Courtesy of Vanessa and Cara.

Sarina's eyes were restless. Among other things, she was taken in by the magic of the night. Rosie had really done a good job. This was nothing short of fantastic. However, with all the awe and admiration pouring out of Sarina's heart, was also a stream of sourness. She flung her eyes across the expanse of tables to the bar, where Elwick was flirting once again with a girl. He had actually gone there to get both himself and Sarina drinks.

Sarina was pulling her eyes away from Elwick when they caught on someone who had just walked into the tent. Her heartbeat spiked and continued to drum in her chest.

Kyan stood at the entrance of the tent, eyes roving, unsure of what to do, or where to go.

Sarina noticed his impeccable dressing. A fitting dark-coloured suit. His hair was flattened backwards. And his ocean eyes, stood out, like two gems.

She was surprised. The last time she had seen him was in the sea, speaking with Ervin. Without legs. Sarina had to admit. He did look good with legs.

Sarina was too engrossed in Kyan to see other girls among the crowd ogle at him.

28

Kyan ran his fingers across the collar of his suit. He stood at the front of the tent, trying to calm his racing heart. People trooped in, chatting, and giggling. He could hear the music from inside.

Soon, Kyan began to grow aware that he was attracting stares. Guess he had stayed out there for too long. He heaved a sigh, his chest rising and falling. Then he walked into the tent.

It was like he had dove into another world. He stood at the mouth of the door, his eyes roving around. He was unsure of what to do next. He made to move further in, when a lady came up to him.

"Hi", she greeted, her pouty lips spreading into a smile.

"Hi", Kyan replied, giving a short nod.

The girl came closer, filling Kyan's nose with the scent of her strong perfume. She blinked rapidly.

"How're you finding the wedding?" she asked. Her voice came out in a croon. "Cool, right?" she supplied, when it seemed Kyan was searching for a reply.

Actually, Kyan had wanted to tell her that he had just come in. Well, the girl supplied an answer herself. It was easier for him to just go with it.

"Yeah, yeah. Cool." He said, nodding in affirmation.

"Yeah?" the girl said, her demeanour brightening.

Kyan looked away, combing through the place for something familiar, more comfortable. Or someone.

The girl leered at Kyan while his eyes were off roaming elsewhere. She took in his blonde hair that flattened backwards to the nape of his neck. His suit wrapped around an athletic body build, and strong arms. She licked her lips, and her eyes burned with predatory desire.

She chuckled.

"What?" Kyan said, flicking his eyes back to her.

She smiled.

"No, I was just speaking, you know, of how Olivia surprised us all. I mean, all this?" she waved her arms gesturing at the insides of the tent. "It's nothing short of… magical."

"Yeah. Magical." Kyan said.

"You know, I, the bride and her sister, we're friends. From

London."

"Oh", Kyan said, nodding in a manner that egged her on, even though he would rather be somewhere else at the moment.

"Now I see why they chose to stay at this... this village. I mean, look at the sea, the beach, the hillside, the flowers, trees." She flicked her eyes towards Kyan and gave him that lecherous look again. "*And the men.*" She added in her mind.

"Uhm..." she began, walking a few inches closer to Kyan, and placing her hand tenderly on his shoulder. "Why don't we get a drink? Or two." Her eyes went suggestively to the bar. "My God, the bar is stacked. Trust me, you'll enjoy it."

Kyan eyes went to the bar. It was stacked alright. Impressive even. But he did not feel like taking a drink with this lady. He was about to revert his gaze to the lady, when a bell went gong! in his head. His eyes flew back, and settled on someone, a guy, chatting with a lady, in a familiar flirtatious manner.

"Elwick." He thought, feeling a surge of revulsion.

Then like a gunshot another thought barged into his mind. "If Elwick was here, that means..."

Kyan eyes flew from Elwick and travelled across the tables until they landed on the long one in front. Now he saw familiar faces. There was Ervin, Olivia, Elan, Rosie, Vanessa...

Then he saw her. His heart pulsated gently. She was quiet, her eyes looking across the tables to the bar, where Elwick was. Kyan could feel her misery. He felt a yearning inside him. Its surge, its tempo, was growing, building to a shriek. He wanted to reach out to her. To wrap her in his arms, and assure her that everything was fine. To draw happiness and peace on her beautiful face. His mind retracted, making the happenings of his immediate surrounding grow into prominence. He heard the sound of talking, and he turned. The girl who had just invited him to a drink was staring softly into his eyes and saying something.

He blinked, coming back fully to himself.

"Huh?" he asked.

"What do you say to a glass of tequila each?"

Kyan looked at Sarina and back again.

"I'm sorry." He said, placing a hand on the girl's shoulder. "It's really nice meeting you, but I can't stay any longer. I've got this thing I've got to attend to."

The girl made to speak, but Kyan had already moved past her. He was too focused on Sarina, he did not see the girls that stared at him with greedy need in their eyes. Or the girl who had just invited him to a drink, walk to a group of girls, say something, then sit. They all watched him as he walked towards the bride and groom's table.

29

Sarina's heart began to race again as she saw Kyan walk closer. She flung her eyes away, creating a pretend-interest in the silver cutlery lying before her.

"Hey. Kyan." She heard someone call from beside her.

"Must be Ervin", she thought.

Voices sprouted from the table, as everyone greeted Kyan. Everyone except Sarina.

Suddenly she felt the presence of someone standing in front. She looked up, and her eyes met Kyan's.

"Hello Sarina"

Sarina stopped her surprise from reflecting on her face.

She thought that after meeting that one time, when she tried fleeing from him, that her name had eroded off his mind as it had been many weeks ago.

"We meet again", Sarina said with a touch of humour.

A little laugh escaped Kyan's mouth.

"How're you enjoying the wedding?" he asked.

Sarina slid her palms down her lap, and back again.

"Pretty well. I get to sit at the big table, you know. The one reserved for the nobles." She said nobles, making a quotation mark with her fingers. "I can count the number of times that has happened to me. Oh, wait a minute." She flung her eyes wide exaggeratedly. "It's never happened to me. This is absolutely my first time." She laughed.

Kyan laughed too.

"Yeah, me too." He said. "This is my first time at a wedding actually."

"Well, this is a beautiful wedding for first times. Just look at the place. A wedding as enchanting as this should be enjoyed."

"Exactly. But I just feel, you know, like I'm sticking out."

"No, you're not," Sarina said with mild indignation. "Did anyone tell you that?"

"Uhhhmmm, no," Kyan replied.

"Hey. Look around you. Just look."

Kyan turned his eyes, allowing them to roam over the place.

"Okay. So what do you see?" she asked.

"Wedding guests, and the celebrants, in suits and dresses."

"Exactly. And you're in a suit, no?"

Kyan smiled. Sarina was awed by the wedding, he could tell. But underlying that was a slather of sadness.

He came close to her, obeying that nudge in his heart.

Just then, the lady occupying the seat beside Sarina left. A thought dropped into Kyan's mind. He appraised the empty seat. Like it was a-once-in-a-life-time opportunity.

"You're right." He said, then looked around. "The wedding is indeed beautiful."

He took a turn around the table and sat in the empty chair.

Now his eyes fell on her, and they talked. It was not necessarily about meaningful things. Just light gist about the sea. How Sarina came to the knowledge of her identity. And how she transformed.

Midway into their conversation, Sarina looked towards the bar. And sighed.

"Is there a problem?" Kyan asked.

"Oh," Sarina said, jerking lightly. "Oh, no. No, no, no. I was just, you know, thinking about how unexpectedly jarring my process of transformation was.''

Her eyes flicked towards the bar again. Elwick was still there, chatting with another girl this time. The one that had approached Kyan earlier. Sarina could wager anything that he had forgotten he had come there to get them drinks.

"Sorry," Kyan said.

She looked at him.

"About your jarring transformation. I wouldn't know anything about that. But yet."

"Oh. That's nothing. It's okay. Moreover, it was totally worth it. Now, I'm a proud mermaid."

"And one that can swim extremely fast too. I mean, you really gave me something for chasing you." He said.

Sarina put her hand to her mouth, to stop a giggle from escaping into public knowledge.

They resumed talking.

There was something, the both of them could tell, coming into fruition between them.

Impulsively, Kyan stretched out his hand as a slow song came on. Sarina's heart was pounding.

"Would you like to dance?" he asked.

Kyan's eyes were firm and solicitous. Sarina's lips spread, creating a beautiful curve on her face.

"Please, no." She said, covering her face with her hands, to hide the flush of embarrassment on her face. "I'm like really bad at dancing. Like I tried those in high school, and I just ended up being a clown rendering free services."

Kyan laughed.

158

"Don't worry", he said. "I'll guide you."

She looked at him, uncertainty dancing in her eyes.

"Just trust me, okay." He said, his eyes kindling with assurance.

Sarina flicked her eyes towards the bar.

"*Yes,*" she said in her mind. "*He's still there chatting.*"

Kyan's hand still hung open right in front of her. Her eyes went around the tent. Everyone was engrossed. Everyone was having a good time.

"Okay." She said, placing her hand on Kyan.

He lifted her hand, and her body followed, rising from the chair.

They walked down to join a couple of dancers, plus the newly wedded couple, on the dance floor. Kyan curled his arm around Sarina's waist, while Sarins's hand rested on his shoulder. The palms of their other hands embraced, and went up, sideways from their bodies. And they danced. In soft graceful steps.

As they danced, they found their eyes amicable pools of brown, in Sarina's case, and greenish-blue, for Kyan.

Kyan was entirely taken in by her. He found her punch-to-the-gut-breathtakingly beautiful. But how to tell her. Her movements were gentle, smooth.

Sarina's mind was light. Like a feather. She was floating among the clouds. Excitement pumping through her, cracking her lips into smiles rich with wishes. She loved the feel of Kyan's arms around her waist, the way he guided her lovingly, like she were a flower. She loved their proximity. Being close to his towering muscular frame, sent jolts through her body. She looked up at him. His eyes were closed. But his mind was there, she could tell, dancing, moving her, like he was making gentle painting strokes on the floor. She also noticed how handsome he looked up close. It was not like he had not been handsome in her eyes before. But now, very close to him, she could appraise, and take in clear descriptions of his handsomeness. His cheekbones were chiselled, like the sea had taken precious time, to gently carve them out. He had a strong jaw. And she noticed how full his lips were. The thought of Kyan's lips suddenly pulled her to Elwick's kissing. Her mind became rife with thoughts of how poor Elwick's kissing was.

Suddenly, something caught her eye from the periphery of her vision. She turned her eyes. And saw Elwick slinking out the tent. His hand was clamped on the girl's wrist that had been talking to him at the bar, and he was pulling her gently along. She heard a roar in her ears and felt her spirits fall so rapidly she hit rock bottom in no time.

Kyan's eyes were looking straight ahead, he did not see the tears that rolled off Sarina's eyes, moistening her makeup, and leaving trails of ruin behind.

"Excuse me", Sarina muttered and extricated herself from Kyan to head out to the washroom in the cottage. She walked out of the tent, leaving Kyan slightly abashed.

Sarina froze, wide-eyed with unbelief, as she burst out of the tent. The scene before her was nothing short of pure outrageous.

30

Two people stood to a corner of the tent's entrance. Their arms were locked, and roving around each other, their bodies mashed together, as they kissed furiously. Sarina recognized Elwick and the girl she had seen him leave the tent with. The girl was an acquaintance of Rosie's. As Elwick groped her, she moaned, passionate sounds that speared through Sarina, tearing out chunks of her heart.

"Elwick", Sarina called, her voice wet with hurt. Tears were streaming out her eyes now.

Elwick froze, flicking his eyes to where Sarina stood, he plucked his lips out from the blonde girl's.

Sarina stared at him, looking into the eyes she had once found loveable.

Elwick made to say something, but Sarina turned and stormed off.

Sarina walked hurriedly, already racking with sobs. She buried her face in her hands as she walked up the familiar path leading to the cottage.

A silhouette extricated itself from the shadows and followed closely behind her. The silhouette moved with purposeful strides, coming closer and closer. Then its hands went into its belt and came out clutching an oblong object. Sarina was close to the cottage now. The silhouette was about a metre or two away from her now. Light from the tent caught against the oblong object and it glinted, just as the silhouette raised it, prepared to strike.

31

Something about the way Sarina left the tent, bugged at Kyan as he stood alone, among a pack of dancing couples. He looked at the doorway, his intuition nagging that he followed her. His eyes flicked across the tent momentarily, and when he was sure that what had just happened was inconspicuous to the wedding guests, turned and walked out of the tent.

Breaking into the night, he noticed a couple making out. His mind flared with anger when he spotted Elwick. His first impulse was to walk over, and sucker punch him. But then something drew his attention away, towards the cottage. His heart skipped. His mind blared. This time not with anger, but with fear and urgency.

He saw Sarina, alright. But there was also something else, or someone. Another harp guard. Moving quickly, closing in on her.

Kyan zapped through the distance like a streak of lightning. In the second it took him to cover the distance, he felt the power of the sea blossoming within him, a nonexpendable bank, reminding him of its presence.

One moment, the harp guard had his arm raised, dagger ready to slice, and the next he was staggering under an influence of a punch to the jaw. Kyan did not give the guard an opportunity for recovery. Quickly, he lurched towards the guard and flung him to the cottage wall. There was a thud on impact, and the guard slid noiselessly to the ground, like a stack of hay. Kyan looked around. None of the wedding guests had noticed as he was some distance away. He looked to where he had last seen Sarina. His eyes caught her just in time, as she took a bend that led away from the house. He made tentative steps towards the guard. Sent a kick to his ribs. But the guard was silent. Satisfied, Kyan knelt beside the guard and muttered the same spell he had used in disposing of the previous one. The guard disappeared. In the exact same manner.

Kyan got to his feet, his shoulders heaving. He looked down towards the beach and caught Sarina going down. He ran after her.

Sarina was engrossed in self-pity and hurt. If she were not a mermaid, she would not have heard the footsteps coming up to her.

She turned, her eyes dripping tears, then turned back and continued walking.

"Hey", Kyan called, walking after her. "Are you alright?"

Sarina was sniffing and sobbing.

Kyan felt a wave of sadness wash over him. It was pretty obvious she was not okay. He gave himself mental reprimands for asking such a question. He stretched his hand, making to touch Sarina when she spoke.

"No", she said in between sobs, "Robert…then…Elwick".

Her tears increased in torrents, and the sobs built into a stuttering cry. She walked hurriedly down to the beach. Kyan froze for a moment. He was sad and hurt, and unsure of what to do. He looked at Sarina crying all alone, in severe pain, and he felt his heart bleed.

He walked quietly to where she stood. Her shoulder racked as she cried. Kyan just stood beside her, silent, for a few moments. Then raising his arm, he coiled it around Sarina's shoulder. Taking the cue, Sarina leaned towards him, placing her head on his shoulder.

They both sat down at the fringes of the beach, the waves lapping at their feet, Kyan's arm nestled around Sarina. Kyan looked into the sea and listened to her cry.

32

The tide had come in a little. The both of them sat, silent as the night sky, as the waves lapped around their feet. However, they did not give a single penny to care. Guess that was one of the quirks of being merpeople.

Sarina traced lines along the surface of the water with her free hand. She loved the way the ripples distorted the reflection of the sky, how the stars would dance until the ripples subsided.

Her head still lay on Kyan's shoulder.

"You know, life can be quite miserable."

"What?" Kyan asked, looking at Sarina.

This was the first coherent sentence she was making, after the incident with Elwick.

"I think", she said, "that some people are just born unlucky."

"You think so?" Kyan asked.

Sarina humphed.

"I know so. I mean look at me. I'm the perfect incarnation of ill luck. I've never truly been in love. All my relationships have ended with me picking up pieces of my heart from the floor. You know," her voice took on a self-righteously piqued tone, "every time, I allow myself to stupidly think I've got it. That I've found true love. I can say what it is. And each time, it slams me right in the face. How unlucky can someone be in ones life?"

She sighed. Kyan listened with rapt attention, eyes fixed on Sarina's face, as she continued.

"Maybe it's because I'm not qualified enough to be loved." Her voice had dropped, taking on a sad self-condescending tone. "I mean who would want to commit to someone like me? Maybe I'm not interesting enough? Or maybe I'm just ugly."

All this while, Kyan was silent. His ears keenly picking up Sarina's words, and his heart feeling them. Hearing Sarina say all these things sparked a runway of emotions that started from disbelief to outright shock.

Kyan found everything Sarina said about herself totally wrong. He looked at her. He could not imagine loving anyone other than her. That was how perfect she was.

"Look, Sarina", he said, extricating himself.

He turned towards her and took both her hands in his.

Sarina sank her brown eyes into his.

"You're wrong, Sarina." He said, fingers interlocked with hers, as he talked.

"What?"

He sighed.

"Everything you just said about yourself is wrong." He said exasperatedly. "You're not ill-fated. Neither are you ugly or not interesting. Sarina, you're the most wonderful thing in the world. Trust me. If the sunset and you were placed side by side, I would pick you. You, Sarina. That's how truly amazing, and beautiful you are." He paused for a moment.

Kyan's voice, his eyes, were heavy with imploring.

Sarina's lungs had gone bereft of air, for about two seconds. And when she finally did breathe, it was in a gush, like the rush of a wind. Kyan caressed her hands with his thumbs, sending threads of pleasure spiking through her hands.

"Really?" Sarina asked, a glitter of excitement shining through her eyes.

Sarina felt a swathe of warmth wrap around her heart, soothing away the hurt, and putting something else there. She felt her heartbeat peak.

Kyan felt the spark too. Kyan parted his lips to speak, but then that was it. Nothing came out. Their level of communication had moved way deeper. They stared into each other's eyes, lost in the pool of emotions they held. The air between them was heavy with the unspoken but said things. It was almost like there had sprung between them a telepathic connection.

Their heads began to droop, coming close to each other. Sarina's eyes went to Kyan's partly open lips. It was like the whole world had gone silent. Like time itself had stopped, and was watching.

33

All of a sudden, Sarina blinked, and stood back, like she had just come out of a daze. Sarina tucked her hair behind her ears.

"You think we should go back to the wedding?" Kyan said, pointing towards the direction of the tent.

"Yeah", Sarina said, blinking. "I just need to use the washroom at the cottage."

"To, you know, clear away the smudged eyeliner and mascara." She added, when she noticed the lost look on Kyan's face.

Kyan oh-ed.

They got up, dusted their clothes, then walked up to the cottage. Kyan stayed out on the porch, waiting for Sarina to go in, do her thing, and come back out.

In Rosie's old room, Sarina dug into her bag and then wiped her face, cleaning off the ruined makeup. Her eyes caught her reflection in the mirror, and she slowed to a stop. She looked at herself for a while, then she sighed, and puffed out air.

"Just look at me." She thought. "Why was I upset about Elwick? I mean, it was clear all along that he had eyes for other girls. Maybe I just didn't want to stand up to the truth. I guess I'd been feeding myself distasteful delusions."

Sarina sighed.

Deep in her heart, she knew all along that she had just had a girly infatuation for him. With him being her assigned protector, his flirtatious manner, he exuded the impression of being the dream.

"But I know better now." She thought.

An image of Kyan blossomed in her mind, filling everywhere, and causing the edge of her lips to tingle till they spread into a smile. She knew that her heart felt more for Kyan than it ever did for Elwick.

"I don't know why I bothered over something that had an underlying of falsehood."

She looked at herself and sighed again. Her hands flew through items, as she reapplied makeup on her face and rearranged her hair.

"Wow. You look stunning, Sarina." Kyan said as she walked out to the porch.

Sarina smiled.

"Thank you, Kyan."

Kyan raised his elbow, and Sarina hooked her arm through. Together they descended the porch and walked towards the tent.

On reaching the tent, Kyan parted the folds for Sarina, allowing her to go in, then he followed in after her.

The place was still lively. It did not notice their absence. At all.

They danced, with lithe movements.

Sarina lapsed into the dance. She felt very comfortable. Happy and excited. As she twirled around and got back to Kyan's arms, her eyes flicked towards the crowd of dancers, and she saw eyes on them.

"Kyan", she whispered.

"Huh?"

"I think we should take a break. Everyone's watching us."

"And?"

"It's just… just…" Sarina stuttered.

"Enjoy the dance" Kyan said. 'Flow with the moment."

Then he leaned into her shoulder, and rested his jaw softly on the flat of her shoulder so that his lips were close to her ear. Sarina found herself smiling uncontrollably. She could not help it. She felt like the luckiest girl in the world.

Kyan's lips began to move, whispering, singing softly into her ear.

''…your name is written in the stars…''

Sarina's eyes perked up. The wheels of Sarina's mind was spinning. She squinted. Her eyes shot wide open.

"You." She said accusingly, looking up at Kyan.

"What?" Kyan asked.

"You..." She said again. Her heart was racing.

Kyan seemed to realize what she was about to say. He sighed. Then bowed his head.

"Yes." He said. "I wrote it."

His eyes had grown soft now and were ripe with emotions. He placed them on Sarina. Sarina looked at him, shock written all over her face.

What Kyan did next, was entirely unexpected.

Swiftly, yet gently, he swooped Sarina from the floor, carrying her in his arms.

Sarina gasped, then wrapped her arms around his neck. Her eyes pierced into his.

"I love you, Sarina. I knew the first moment I saw you, in the sea. It was the spark you ignited in my heart that made me decide to become a landwalker. Should you wish to live on the land or sea, I will be there Sarina… My love for you will never die."

Sarina could not control the influx of excitement. She tightened her arms around Kyan's neck and placed her face into his chest.

Then their heads leaned into each other, their foreheads touching and forming a pyramid between their faces. They stayed that way for a few seconds, in which time, everything had slowed down for them. It was just the sound of their heartbeats, their breathing, and their eyes staring into each other's.

Sarina's lips parted. Then Kyan tilted his head slowly. And they both went in for a kiss.

Whoops and applause broke out in the tent. Sarina and Kyan broke out the kiss, stared at themselves, then started laughing, radiant smiles adorning their faces, and everyone's in the tent. It was a beautiful sight.

Olivia walked to where Rosie was standing watching Kyan and Sarina with excitement and nudged her.

Rosie turned, smiling.

"Look who's found her merman," Olivia said.

Rosie laughed.

"Looks like the mermaid family is growing. Quintess best watch out." She said.

"Hell yeah," Olivia said.

The tempo of the music increased, and then there was general clapping, in two successive quick beats, accompanying the instruments. The newlyweds moved to the dance floor and danced to the beat. Kyan and Ervin exchanged smiles. As did Sarina and Olivia. Rosie moved in with Elan. Vanessa with Adian.

As they danced, they began to chant along, stomping their feet on the ground. This was joy. This was beauty. The beauty of wild love.

Meanwhile, amongst the celebrations nobody had noticed
that a shadowy figure of a man crept alongside the tent… or
that Cara was not amongst them celebrating… that she had
been gone too long and had not returned… apart from one
man growing concerned by the minute… stood amongst the
wedding guests… a man who was secretly a merman, a
resident of Cliffside, who had hidden his identity, from
everyone he knew, his entire life…

Thank you for reading **Wild Love**

Did you like the book? I'll be forever grateful if you take the time to leave a quick star rating or review.

Reviews are the number one way you can help other people discover new authors, and each and every review supports us on our journey to bring you more stories.

WANT MORE?

Wild Hope – Book Five of the Mermaids of Cornwall Series

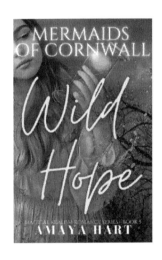

THE FOLLOWING IS AN EXCERPT FROM BOOK 5 - WILD HOPE:

The Blakely family had first arrived in Cliffside, a year or two ago. They had come in a red Audi A4, and a truck in tow. They had driven through the village, piquing the interest of every villager they passed, till they had stopped in front of a two-storey house.

Ms. Blakely had stepped out of the car, opened the door for a twelve year old Cara and a fifteen year old Vanessa stepped out from the other side. They stood in front of the house, looking at it, like they were trying to bring themselves to tell it a heartfelt goodbye. Only in this case, it would be more like a 'hi'.

The breeze that day had combed furiously through Cara's free-falling hair, buffeting it, and causing it to whip around her face. Somehow the twelve year old did not care. Her face was blank, and her eyes searching. She combed through the humble house that stared back at her. A mockery of their house back in London.

"This is our home now", her mother had said, then squeezed their hands affectionately. "Vanessa", her mother had called, "Watch after your little sister, will you."

Vanessa flicked her hair and then turned to watch their mother move towards the little truck that carried bits of their properties from their old home. She sighed and then turned towards her little sister.

"Hey, sis." She said, "Want to sit?"

Cara did not turn. She did not move.

"No", she replied.

And that was it. For a moment or so.

Vanessa had stood by her little sister, unsure of what to do. She placed her hand on Cara's shoulder and made to speak, when Cara spoke,

"I want to go back."

The words stunned Vanessa. They had been totally unexpected. Direct from the blue.

"What?' she asked.

Cara turned to her. Her eyes swirled with anger, but it was anger tempered with longing, and dislike.

"I want to go back to London." She said.

Vanessa flicked her eyes towards their mother who was busy giving directions to the men offloading properties from the truck. Then she looked back to her sister, sighing with resignation. The task unanimously fell to her.

"We can't go back to London, Cara." She said, making sure to water down her voice with as much affection as could moisten a rock.

"Why not?" Cara asked, her voice thick with conviction. She sent her eyes down the street, and an almost empty, very sleepy street stared back. Without shame.

"Mum has a reason for bringing us out here."

"Mhm? What's that?"

Vanessa stared into the air for some seconds, but came back empty.

"Okay look", she said, taking Cara by the hand, and leading her to the foot of the stairs that led to the door of their new house. She sat, and with a slight tug, led Cara to sit beside her.

"I don't know why mum decided that it would be nice for us to move from London. You can ask her when she'd one with arrangements. But here's something. You can tell me why you want to go back to London."

Cara looked down the street again. Once in a while, a villager would walk past. Even rarer, a string of two or three villagers. All of them would trudge by, silently, like an enormous weight was on their shoulders, and keeping quiet would help conserve energy. All of them cast curious glances at the newbies. Glances that could easily pass off as one of disinterest or cold hostility.

"Look at this place, Vanessa. It's so quiet. There are no parks. No huge tall buildings. No cars, no nothing."

Vanessa shut her eyes. Then opened them calmly.

"I know, Cara." She replied, holding her sister's hands in hers, and running her thumbs across the back. "But look at the bright side. Here there is an abundance of wild, naturally cultured plant

181

life. I mean, we could take walks through the hills, you can feel the green, the flowers. It's really beautiful, Cara."

Cara looked at her sister and flung her eyes away, unconvinced.

"Ooh," Vanessa said, her face brightening. "There are also beaches, Cara. Beautiful ones, in different places around the village. We could go there, you know, hang out, and bathe in the sun. Build sandcastles, if you want. That's something you won't see in London."

Vanessa finished her statement with the rush of victory one had after spewing out a damning string of argumentative points.

Cara pouted, then turned to the side to sulk in peace. Vanessa sighed exasperatedly. She got up, beat her palms across her backside to rid it off clingy particles of dust. Then she moved towards the truck to go stand by her mother.

Even time in the village seemed to go by in a drawl. Cara felt like an invisible cloak of drowsy pressure was around her, trying to make her go under. And she was only a few inches above from that. From under. She missed her friends back in London. The funny games they would play during school. The get-togethers they organised at each other's homes. Wonderful. Here, there was nothing. But quiet and boredom.

It all took a sharp swerve for the better when she happened upon Joshua, one day, while in the village market with her mother.

They had had a shortage of vegetables at home, and so there

was a need for a refill. Vanessa was off doing something, and so the duty of accompanying had fallen on Cara. She had clutched the empty brown wicker basket her mother had brought for carrying the vegetables, fit her feet into light brown leather sandals, and towed after her mother, albeit morosely.

The market was a lukewarm cluster of stalls. Products were arranged out on stands. They looked lonely and forlorn. It was super easy for a complacent Cara to glaze over them like they never existed. Her mother stopped by a vegetable stall and began to exchange words on prices with the seller. It was while she stood there, bored to near-death, wiggling her toes for fun that someone bumped into her.

Cara had looked up sharply, shooting a cold stare, when her eyes faltered. They seemed to flicker in and out, uncertain of whether to stay cold, or to assume warmth, or some other variation of warmth; since she did not know the boy that was standing before her.

Joshua stood almost a head taller than her, and his 'sorrys' came out in pelts.

"I wasn't looking." He said. "The carrots were so good."

Unable to help herself, Cara laughed, clutching a hand to the base of her stomach. The sound, coming from her, was like an eccentric peal sundering the soup-ish quiet of the place. It prompted her mother to break out from her conversation with the seller and cast an alarming look her way. The look of alarm, quickly melded into a satisfied smile, when it came in fully that her daughter was smiling.

"Hm. A friend", Mrs. Banks thought, as she looked back to the seller, and pointed at an array of lettuces, "that's just what she needs, eh?"

"Carrots? Really?" Cara spluttered, still heavily influenced by hilarity.

"Yeah. Carrots." Joshua said, raising his eyes to buttress his truth.

But Cara only laughed some more.

"Hey come on", he said, "you better stop laughing. Death by laughter is punishable here."

Cara's breath caught in her throat, and then a torrent of laughter came rushing out. Joshua joined in this time.

"Hi. I'm Joshua." He introduced himself after their laughing spell was over.

"And I'm Cara."

BOOKS BY AMAYA HART

Mermaids of Cornwall Series – pick up the next book:

Prequel – Wild Witch

Book 1 - Wild Hearts

Book 2 - Wild Dreams

Book 3 - Wild Soul

Book 4 - Wild Love

Book 5 - Wild Hope

Book 6 – Wild Magic

KEEP IN TOUCH

Would you like to connect?

I love chatting with readers.

You can email me on: **amaya.hart@outlook.com**

We will NOT share, sell or spam your email. You will only receive an email when there is a new book release or during sneak peeks.

Made in United States
Orlando, FL
09 September 2023

36858543R00119